Plague of the Sky Spores!

He waved the loaded syringe in front of him like a knife. The men parted uncertainly, opening a path to the wards. He waited for one of them to pull a hero act, but no one tried anything.

Linda lay in a bed in the middle of the crowded ward, fighting the restraints that bound her arms and legs.

Rob pulled her sheets aside and swabbed an area just below her navel.

"Forgive me," he sobbed, as he plunged the needle in.

VECTOR ANALYSIS

Jack C. Haldeman II

A BERKLEY BOOK
published by
BERKLEY PUBLISHING CORPORATION

A portion of this novel first appeared in *Analog*,
copyright © 1977 by Conde Nast Publications, Inc.

This Berkley book contains the complete
text of the original hardcover edition.
It has been completely reset in a type face
designed for easy reading, and was printed
from new film.

VECTOR ANALYSIS

A Berkley Book / published by arrangement with
the author

PRINTING HISTORY
Berkley-Putnam edition published December 1978
Berkley edition / January 1980

ISBN: 0-425-04275-8

A BERKLEY BOOK® TM 757,375
Berkley Books are published by Berkley Publishing Corporation.
PRINTED IN THE UNITED STATES OF AMERICA

Acknowledgments

The seeds of this book go back a long way. I am greatly indebted to Dr. Everett L. Schiller of the Department of Pathobiology, Johns Hopkins University, Baltimore, Maryland. Mentor and advisor, he, along with my parents, fostered and nurtured a love and understanding within me for biology and the interrelationships of living systems.

Thanks also to David Hartwell of Putnam/Berkley, Ben Bova of *Analog* Magazine, and Kirby McCauley, literary agent. Their advice, patience and friendship was a great help. Thanks also to Vol, for love and understanding.

Jack C. Haldeman II
New Port Richey, Florida, 1978

Chapter One

They soared, the mountains rose behind them, rough jagged crests framing a huge ball of orange fire. Twin moons hung low in the western sky. The desert stretched out below them; sweeping patterns of wind-blown sand, small plants, stunted trees casting long shadows in the morning light. They flew together, a habit from long years of association, gently catching the thermals, crossing the edge of the desert in long, sweeping curves. Their multifaceted eyes scanned the ground, alert for movement, alert for food. Occasionally they communicated with a sound that was a cross between a squawk and a wail. It bounced between canyon walls, echoed out across the desert floor.

They were lords of their planet, kings of wind and storm. In the air they were invincible, without enemies. Only on the ground did they know danger. They could stay aloft for hours, drifting, coasting with barely perceptible movements of their flattened bodies.

Mantas, a touch of pterodactyl. Skimming the high winds in the morning sun, they looked more like manta rays from Earth than anything else. Yet they were built for the sky, not water; the sky was their home, the air their domain. Even with a wing span of over twelve meters, they weighed less than ninety kilograms. Their bones were hollow reeds, their skin tough, lightweight. Moving with a fluid grace, their bodies caught and reflected the early sun, their shadows chased each other across the warming sand.

The planet had a name, a number, a certain list of characteristics and coordinates carefully recorded in books and computers back on Earth. It had been identified, catalogued, photographed, and scanned by remote probes. It hung in the minds of men who were concerned with such things like an insect skewered on a pin, tucked away in a box stuffed with cotton. The mantas knew nothing of this and wouldn't have cared. They were secure, dominant. They knew only of food, thirst, hunger, warmth, cold; physical needs and conditions that were either satisfied or endured. They were static creatures, living their lives in unhurried routine. How different they were from the warm-blooded, furry animals they fed upon, rapid quadrapeds that scuttled on the ground with hearts that beat too fast and lives that were too short.

Other creatures shared the sky with the mantas, neither food nor threat, ignored. Near the ground small animals flew, insects buzzed. Higher, where the air grew thin and cold, the gossamer, jellyfish-like organisms twisted and drifted their lives away, breaking apart and reforming at will. They were nearly transparent, insubstantial. The mantas often passed directly through their bodies, with no harm to either.

Often flying along with the mantas were small, feathery creatures that looked like a cross between a butterfly and a suction cup. They would adhere to various places on the manta's skin and scoop small organisms from the air as they rode along. The mantas ignored them. They were trivial, below notice.

The wheel of evolution was slowly turning on this named and numbered planet, the manta's days were dying out. This, like the presence of man in some other corner of the universe, was of little concern to them. Their awareness was one of the wind, the rising sun, the smell of showers in from the east.

The male saw it first, a split second before his mate. A shadow movement a kilometer or more away; a short, jerky movement that meant food. In unison, they banked to the left and began a swift and silent descent.

In the shadows on the still cool sand, the furry mammal, like the mantas above him, was looking for food. In his case it was grubs, berries on the sharp-thorned plants, small crunchy things that burrowed in the sand. Finding a small nest of swarming insects he had become excited, overcome by the desire to feed. He pushed the sand away with his forepaws, rooted deeper with his long snout. Blindly feeding, he became careless, stepped into the sun. It was this action that had pinpointed him to the mantas, the shadow that was a trail, an arrow pointing directly at him.

He never had a chance.

The male had dropped back as usual, so the female

hit him first, a glancing blow with her unsheathed talons that sent the small creature sprawling across the sand. Before he had stopped rolling, the male manta had lifted him into the air with a grip that closed around his chest like a vise.

On this primitive world life was a fragile thing, death was the rule. The unwary died suddenly. The cautious died slowly. The difference was survival in life's most basic terms—the ability to live, to reproduce, to perpetuate the species. Swinging in the sky, the small, dead bundle of fur had lost his battle, his one chance. His kind was adaptable and might yet rule the planet, but for now it was the manta's turn, and as they headed back to the roost to feed, they knew no fear.

And because they knew no fear it was with curiosity more than alarm that they viewed the strange new sun burning out of the sky. It wasn't food, couldn't possibly be danger, not in the sky.

As the probe ensnarled them in its plexi-steel net, they struck out with rage. They only started to feel fear as it slowly drew them into the opening in its belly. By then it was too late.

The small mammal, forgotten and released in the struggle, fell through the gaps in the net and tumbled to the desert floor. Its body would be devoured by the grubs it had been feeding upon.

Inside the probe the two men worked quickly and efficiently. After six months of orbiting the planet they had finally collected all their specimens. They had also mapped nearly every square kilometer of the planet's surface and sent down twelve ground probes, unmanned mobile scientific stations. Eleven had functioned perfectly, with only spectographic data missing from the twelfth. The amount of information they gathered in such a short period of time was staggering; even they were impressed at how smoothly things had gone. Besides being stored in the on-board computers, all their data had been relayed to a satellite placed in orbit beyond the second moon. Insurance, in case anything happened to the two men. Everything had a back-up system.

Even allowing for the required margin of safety, the men were cutting things close. Collecting specimens of dominant species was the last thing on their mission profile and they wanted to do it right. A mated pair! They were more than satisfied.

Already dubbed mantas, the two animals had been subdued and restrained. Snug in the belly of the probe, they were surrounded by a slowly thickening gel that would cushion them against the acceleration forces they would soon encounter.

One of the men was busy punching numbers into the computer while the other floated across the room working from a checklist strapped to his left wrist. They worked silently, without talking. They had been together a long time and all the little bits of conversation had been exhausted. The mission was all that remained and their part in it was almost over.

In roughly three hours and twenty-seven minutes they would fire the large rockets that would take them out of orbit and accelerate them towards the distant rendezvous point. There, the ion-drive mother ship would pick them up on its swing back towards Earth. They were one of eight manned probes the ship had dropped like eggs around various selected planets on its outward loop. The ship would snatch the probe on its flyby much as the probe had snatched the mantas.

* * *

Rob McGreggor slid his bunk into the wall and flipped down the chair in front of his desk. Forms, forms, and more forms; bureaucratic nonsense he thought he'd left behind on Earth. No such luck. Date of birth, maternal great-grandfather's date of birth, color of father's eyes, number of miscarriages, history of multiple births—what? Oops, wrong section. He wrote DOES NOT APPLY in block letters across the page. He did this with great satisfaction and underlined it twice.

He attacked the remaining pages with a determined vengeance, pausing only to fix himself a cup of instant coffee. It wouldn't be so bad if this had anything to do with his research, but it was all just general information. He considered it something of a rite of passage, a mountain of paper to surmount before he could get down to business. His second day on Delta III and all he'd done since he arrived was get poked by a dozen doctors and move a lot of papers around. The folder of forms in front of him was quite thick in spite of the tissue-thin paper. He supposed Linda had a hand in some of the questionnaires, but the thought didn't cheer him. He finished the last page and signed his name for what seemed to be the thousandth time. His coffee was cold and he poured the remains down the drain in his small sink.

His cubicle was small and tidy, almost sterile. He'd brought up very few personal items, hadn't come close to filling his personal weight allotment. No pictures, photographs; the only luxury he allowed himself was a small a/v cassette playback unit with headphones. It sat on his dresser with the screen popped up, a stack of micro-cassettes beside it. The screen was projecting a page from one of his texts, a

biochemical flow sheet he'd been studying earlier. A
few of his cassettes were music or popular novels,
mostly mysteries by two or three favorite authors,
but the majority were reference works pertaining to
his research. His grant would only last nine months
to a year and he figured he'd be busy most of the
time. The multicolored flow sheet glowed in the
corner of his cubicle like a painting or a holo on
someone else's wall.

Rob had been shuttled up to work on the last
stages of his Ph.D. project, supported by a grant
from the World Health Organization with matching
funds from the National Science Foundation.
National and international funds were often mixed to
offset the considerable expense of working in space.
Delta III, the newest of the fourth generation orbiting stations, had been especially designed for
biological and medical research.

He worked on schistosomes, small parasites that
lived in the bloodstreams of man, weakening him,
robbing him of energy and making him more susceptible to other diseases. The intermediate host, or
vector, of this parasite was a common snail. All too
common, as it turned out. With the recent
reclamation and extensive irrigation of what had
once been the Sahara Desert, the snail population
had increased and the problems had mushroomed. In
certain portions of the world it had reached epidemic
proportions and Rob was just one of many working
on it.

Even though he was still a relatively young man,
Rob was well prepared to undertake his own in-
dependent research project. He was a product of the
still experimental Accelerated Education Program,
the latest in a long series of attempts to streamline

and make more effective the educational process. He had graduated from pre-med at seventeen, went through med school in three years, specializing in physiology. Then, following an obligatory two-year U.N. stint, he had decided to specialize in pathobiology, concentrating on parasitology. His Masters degree had come quickly and it was while he was working on his thesis and field work on amoebic dysentery that he became interested in schistosomes. It was a fortunate decision since it soon became a popular disease, like cancer had once been, and funding was relatively easy to come by.

It was fascinating and taxing work. He loved it. He'd always considered himself something of a dabbler, picking up small bits of information from various places and trying to fit them together. As a child, he'd been fascinated by puzzles. Parasitology was a perfect outlet for that. Not only did he have to know everything possible about the parasite, but he had to have a working knowledge of the physiology of both the intermediate and final hosts, in this case as dissimilar as man and snail. In addition he often delved into other branches of scientific discipline— botany, to see how the snails fed; ecology, to see how the changes brought about by the irrigation had shifted the snail's patterns; pharmacology, biochemistry, etc., etc. He often found himself as far afield as the physics of water currents and the complicated plumbing of sanitary engineers and mammalian uro-genital systems. He was still a kid playing with puzzles but now he was getting paid for it.

On Delta III Rob would be able to study the schistosomes and their snail vectors in a way impossible on Earth. Here he could control almost every conceivable factor: gravity, heat, light, atmosphere.

Maybe the answer would be there, maybe only new data added to the constantly growing bank of scientific knowledge. He had designed his experimental protocol carefully and it passed the board with only minor changes and additions. Accordingly, it could be carried out nowhere else but on Delta III. The fact that Linda was also on a year's tour here hadn't entered into it at all.

Rising, Rob gathered up all the papers, stuffed them in the folder and flicked off his desk lamp. He had pushed the privacy screen aside before he realized he'd left the viewer on. He walked back across the cubicle—it only took four steps—and started to turn it off, paused a moment. He pushed the scan button and held it down as images slid across the screen. He stopped at a new chart, hit the intensifier and magnified a portion of it. The Krebs cycle . . . glucose triosephosphate, pyruvic acid. He studied it for a moment, although he knew it by heart, then turned off the machine. It was fresh in his mind now, and he knew his subconscious would mull it over for a while, follow random connections while he did other things. It was a habit he picked up as a kid working crossword puzzles. The answers often popped into his head hours later while he was thinking of something else. He trusted his subconscious, it didn't stumble around as his conscious mind did. He left his cubicle, headed towards the corridor.

He had to return the forms to Johnson, the personnel coordinator. Her office was on the other side of the station, and while he could go the long way around and stay at one-g, it was quicker to cut across. Besides, he'd have to get used to the shifting gravity sometime. He still felt clumsy and awkward at anything but one-g and none too graceful there.

As he left the men's quarters, the corridor widened and branched out into the biosector. Rob decided to take that route even though it wound around a lot and was quite a bit longer. He was still exploring the station, feeling his way around. The orientation tour yesterday had been so rapid and superficial it had done nothing but confuse him. Everywhere he went he seemed to bump into people. The station was a lot larger than he'd expected. So many people, still strangers, all with their jobs, their own responsibilities. He felt lost in the shuffle.

His own lab was located in the biosector, a wedge of the station that started out at one-g and fanned into the zero-g area, comprising almost a third of the entire station. Rob's individual lab was a small one located in the one-g section, still filled with unopened packing crates. He also had access to the general purpose labs at any desired gravity. The biosector was honeycombed with small compartments, all connected by shifting corridors. The one he was currently going down led him past the exobiologists' center.

Rob smiled as he passed one of the harried technicians in the corridor. Exobiology had taken a quantum jump with the arrival of *Pegasus* a few months ago. Before that most of their work had been theoretical except for a few limited, primitive samples from Mars and Venus. Now they had a lot of new material to play with and they were still at the stage of sorting things out. There was a sense of excitement and urgency that permeated the whole area; a situation where unexpected breakthroughs were happening almost daily.

Although the specimens were effectively isolated, it was possible to view them along the corridor through one-way portholes and monitors that dotted their enclosures. Some of them, like the mantas, had large viewing areas set aside with chairs and benches. At 0.7-g Rob passed by one such compartment. It contained some sort of creature that adhered to the surrounding rocks with thousands of small suckers. The animals were thin and rubbery, with the general surface appearance of the rocks themselves. They were also very sluggish and, as Rob had noticed the day before, very boring to watch.

Down the corridor a short distance, in the 0.5-g section, were the mantas. Rob felt a bit giddy as he grabbed the railing, settled into one of the vacant chairs. He was grateful for the chance to rest a moment, to let his body adjust to the lesser gravity. He was tired of overestimating his movements and bumping into things, half staggering, half floating.

As he watched the mated pair, they hung upside down from supports in their enclosure like bats, seemingly asleep. *Alien,* so strange. Very much like something that might have lived on Earth and yet at the same time so . . . well, so *different,* as if shaped by alien hands or formed in the mind of a madman. He wondered if the butterflies in with them could be considered parasites. If not, he wondered if the mantas had parasites at all and if they did, whether he would be able to recognize them as such.

They hung there, unmoving, and he watched them for a short while, thinking of the popular reports that had made the newsfax when they arrived. He tried to picture their world, how they must have looked when they lived there. He had seen pictures, the holos, the maps. He'd read the specifications of their planet and could reel off the information from memory, but somehow it didn't connect. He couldn't imagine the

mantas anywhere else but in this cubicle, a metal and
glass test tube. He thought of them as specimens, like
the creatures frozen on microscope slides in his lab
and for a moment it worked. Yet there was
something else, something he couldn't quite put his
finger on, something powerful, almost mystical. It
probably had something to do with being in the
presence of something so totally alien that even
dreams and nightmares had more touches of reality.
It gnawed at him, bothered him, so he rose to leave.

The male manta stretched, unfolding one huge
wing, and seemed to regard Rob with an eye that
glowed like a cold green jewel. Rob shuddered and
quickly headed down the corridor.

When he reached Johnson, she handed him
another set of forms with an engaging smile. Rob
didn't even try to manage a polite smile in return. He
was beginning to suffer from terminal writer's cramp.

Short cropped gray hair, stocky, muscular with
hard lines etched into a granite face: Captain Riggs
shifted slightly in his form-fitted chair, tapping but-
tons set in the ends of his armrests under his fingertips. The screens in front of him flickered, blinked. It
was all rote, automatic. He sat at the nerve center of
Delta III, sorting out the complex array of readouts
and vidscreens into one smooth flowing unit. He
sensed, as much as read, the patterns that they
traced; patterns that monitored every aspect of the
station. Intuitively, he could tell if anything was even
marginally wrong by bumps in the patterns, usually
before the actual causes flashed across the board.
Today there were no real bumps, everything was
smooth.

Tucker Riggs they used to call him, for some

reason he could never understand; his first name was Robert, Bob, but for a brief moment in front of the console he was Tucker again, fair-haired flyboy, the last of a dying breed. There had been an olive branch on each wingtip of his silver death machine. *Peacekeeping*. A war was a war, a place where men died, the words they chose to label it with didn't matter. It had been a hot summer in a small African country. The U.N. paid him well, it was just before he met Marsha. He had been a good pilot, methodical, cool-headed when others were gripped in panic. There were some medals, awards. It had been a good time for him but then, he had been young. That had a lot to do with it. If the U S hadn't lured him into space with the promise of command, he'd probably still be wearing the blue and white. Flying a desk, most likely. Pushing papers around. He adjusted the focus on one of the monitors.

There was a rhythm to the hidden life on the station, complex cadences that flowed through the board. Riggs flowed with them; shifting consumables around, keeping track of essential services. Like a symphony conductor, he kept a thousand bits of business in his head at the same time. He was seldom actually aware of it, it was simply his job. He was good at it. He sensed a movement behind his back.

That would be Ed Brown, second in command. He was two and a half minutes early. Riggs acknowledged his premature presence with a curt nod of his head, never taking his eyes off the screens, the dials. Sorting himself out, he took care of a few loose ends, rather than leave them for the next shift. He liked a tidy board. Everything was green. He flashed an end of shift update to Delto II where it would be automatically stored.

He heard Brown ease into his chair, felt it hum into life. Brown was duplicating his actions, getting into sync with the flow of data. Riggs punched a pattern on the center screen. Brown matched it instantaneously. They were linked, for a moment they moved in unison. Riggs felt his controls go dead as his seat swiveled away from the board and Brown's slid into place. He mentally shifted gears. He was off duty. As off duty as a commander could ever be with the responsibility for 200 lives constantly on his shoulders. He left the control room without a word.

Couldn't Brown ever be *exactly* on time?

Riggs washed his face with cold water in his room and headed towards the canteen for lunch. Lunch was the only meal he didn't have sent to his quarters. He felt that it was necessary to eat with the crew once a day. It kept up the appearances of availability even though he was always surrounded by the same people, the same officers. It fit into his daily pattern and the pattern became habit.

With a slight wince he remembered that his routine would be broken in a couple weeks or so. Some hotshot politician was talking about coming up. Usually he let Brown take care of the VIPs and visiting firemen, but it had been suggested by Ground Control that he roll out the red carpet for this one, show him around himself. Anything less would be a snub. Politics! He hated politicians, they were all slippery as hell. Maybe he could get away with a couple of quick tours, give him dinner in the captain's quarters and hand him over to Brown. Brown was better in dealing with people anyway, a talent he himself had never bothered to cultivate.

Besides, he was a busy man and couldn't afford to break his routine.

His routine: eight hours on the board, comprised of two four-hour shifts, and sixteen hours off. In his off-time he spent an hour and a half eating, three hours excercising, eight hours sleeping, and three and a half hours to himself—reading, conversing with the crew, keeping appointments, taking care of miscellaneous affairs. He would have to fit the senator in under miscellaneous affairs. The crew considered Riggs a creature of habit. They said you could set your watch by the time he shaved in the morning. You could.

He entered the canteen. It was precisely 1300 hours. His lunch was waiting, warm. It had been set down at his customary place two minutes previously by a crew member who was also a creature of the captain's habits.

Linda Shaw was sweating hard, glad the match was nearly over. Spinning slowly, she swung at the ball, connected. Rob frantically kicked off in a vain effort to intercept it before the fourth rebound. Had he managed to reach it he would have found Linda in a perfect position to send it back. As it was, he misjudged again and ended up in an awkward spin that bought him to rest abruptly against the far wall.

It was unfair and she knew it. She had been playing almost every day for three months and Rob was still relatively new to the station, unused to zero-g sports. But she played games, like she did everything else, to the best of her abilities.

Rob served to her and she nailed him to the wall. Final point.

Following tradition, Rob floated to mid-court to congratulate her. He did this with a couple of very non-traditional squeezes. She responded with a playful grab, which he managed to avoid and a shake of her head, which he couldn't.

"Not tonight," she said. "Early duty."

"Lunch tomorrow, then," Rob said, feeling only slightly put down. Actually, he was exhausted and still had to make some adjustments to the heat increment stage of his experiment.

Linda reached behind her neck and unfastened her barette, releasing a cloud of long blond hair that floated around their faces, brushing, tickling, sensuous. They held each other loosely for a moment, drifting slowly, movements causing movements. She almost changed her mind. Early duty, she reminded herself with a kick that spiraled them towards the exit.

Tomorrow she would be working with Dr. Turner and he always started early. It was time to administer the post-tour psychological profiles on the members of the crew rotating down on the next shuttle. The examinations were of her own design and she was proud of them. Actually, she looked forward to working with Turner. Unlike most of her colleagues in clinical psychology, he actually seemed to care about people.

Outside the women's section they lingered, made plans for the next day, separated.

All Linda wanted was a shower and some sleep. She preferred the one-g showers, never felt really clean after the zero-g ones. They were fun once in a while, though, especially with a friend. Lots of soap and slippery giggles.

She walked quietly past the darkened cubicles. Soft laughter came from behind Maria's curtain, muffled noises of people moving around. That would most likely be Julia, Maria's current lover. There were no secrets on Delta III.

Linda had considered taking a lover when she first came up. There had been lots of offers, both male and female, and she had been tempted. Now she was glad she hadn't given in; it would have complicated matters. Things were good with Rob, had been good since they were kids together in pre-med.

Rob kept trying to talk her into sharing a cubicle with him. It might be nice, probably would be, but she liked things better the way they were. She occasionally stayed over with him, but for reasons she didn't quite understand it was necessary that she keep her own cubicle, her own existence, a little separate for now. Maybe later.

Her cubicle was littered with papers and charts, they covered her desk and most of her bunk, overflowed into loose stacks on the floor. She did a lot of her paperwork here, partly because it was quiet, but mostly because of the privacy. In her office people were always barging in, wanting to talk, just pass the time, flirt. It was hard to turn them down tactfully, get rid of them, and equally hard to get any work done.

At least in the cubicle it was possible to get some privacy. By an unwritten rule no one entered if a person's screen was shut. It was about the only way to be alone in the entire station.

Linda stripped off her clothes, leaned outside to toss them into the pick-up in the corridor. She pulled at her sweat-tangled hair for a moment, frowned into the mirror and grabbed a tube of shampoo off her shelf. Moving papers around, she found a clean towel, wrapped it around her and headed for the showers.

"How'd the match go?" It was Jodie Pope, a technician who worked with Rob.

"Twenty-one to zero." They walked together down the corridor. Linda was taller, more heavily built, solid without being overly muscular. Sports activities had been a regular part of her life since her childhood in rural Iowa. She carried it well. Jodie, on the other hand, couldn't have weighed more than a hundred pounds carrying two sacks of groceries. She was small, too; not more than 4'10". She burned up energy like crazy, had never been able to put on weight.

"Hope he'll recover," said Jodie. "We've got lots to do tomorrow."

"I think he'll live," she said with a laugh. "The guy's got stamina."

She had stayed on the courts too long. There were three other people in the shower and the water was cold.

Senator Arnold Greer sneaked a glance at his digital; 1400 hours on the button. After nine years of practice, his timing was, as usual, perfect. He'd read his prepared statement and allowed as little time as possible for questions. His limousine stood nearby. Five minutes and he'd have to leave. The shuttle couldn't wait. You can't rush a launch window. Balancing cameras on their shoulders and pushing microphones forward, the reporters crowded around him, jostling each other for a better position.

"Senator, is there any truth to the rumors that your subcommittee is going to recommend a total halt to government funding of the Delta series?"

That was Bill Watson of United Network. Greer was well aware that he'd get good coverage from

United, so he picked that question out of the many that were being thrown at him.

"Well, Bill, let's just say that our feeling is that the previous two administrations have overcommitted themselves in the area of basic research. We simply aren't getting enough benefits to justify the expense."

"Do you have any comment on the report in this morning's *Times* that you have already reached a decision, that your visitation will only be a formality?"

"Not true. I'm simply going up to get my information first hand, to get a *feel* of the situation, so to speak. There have been no decisions, and especially no private deals. I don't know where the *Times* gets their misinformation these days. Can't even trust their sports pages."

"What about your public criticism of Operation Snatch? People are saying that you're not objective enough to head the committee, much less be the one to make the investigation." That was Otis Weekfield, a troublemaker and first-class nuisance. Unfortunately, he also wrote a widely syndicated column.

"You know me better than that, Otis," Greer said, flashing the innocent grin that had carried him through so many close elections. "Project *Pegasus*, or Operation Snatch, as you so informally called it, has been a success, nobody's questioning that. Our knowledge of the universe has increased tremendously. But at what cost, I ask you, what cost? Militarily we are barely holding our own, if indeed we haven't fallen behind already. My only objection with Project *Pegasus* is that it could just as well have been undertaken by private concerns using private money and left the government free to use its money to serve and protect its people. This, however, is water under the bridge, finished business. It in no way influences the investigation my committee is currently undertaking.''

Otis indeed knew Greer better than that, but his rebuttal was lost in the clamor for additional questions. Otis simmered. Most of the things he knew about Greer he couldn't print. Otis may have won the Pulitzer five years ago for investigative reporting, but he also had a strong desire to keep breathing and Greer had some very heavy friends. Someday, he'd put Greer's ass in a sling.

Looking into the crowd, Greer picked out Richard Corona from the news, the one with the planted question. He pointed a finger at him.

"Senator Greer, how long do you anticipate this visit to take?''

"The purpose of a fact finding mission is to find facts,'' *there*, the quote for this afternoon's headlines, "and I'll stay as long as necessary, visiting all three Delta series stations. Besides, it'll give me a chance to get away from all you rascals for awhile,'' the joke, put them in good humor.

"Thank you gentlemen, I'm afraid that's all the time I have for questions. Shuttles don't wait for senators, you know.'' The grin again, a wave, pause for the cameras to get a little more background film and then into the air-conditioned limo and out to Kennedy Space Center for the lift. Damn nuisance.

Greer stared through the tinted glass at the scrubby palmettos and marsh grass passing by. The electric engine was soundless, he was separated from the driver and Mike Hickson, his aide, by a thick glass plate. The air conditioning hissed quietly, soothingly. What a desolate place to put the shuttle. Nothing civilized for miles. He thought of the political manipulations that had caused it to be built here in the first place and smiled. Even back then they had known how to play the game.

It was a game, after all, only a game—but the stakes were tremendously high. He hadn't spent the last eight years doing scut work in the Senate for nothing. Contacts, thousands of contacts nurtured over cocktail glasses in ivy-covered patios behind Georgetown houses. Smoke-filled rooms, under-the-table money and bargains were the key to the game and Greer had learned the ropes very well. He felt like a juggler, balancing several shifting relationships at the same time. A lot of people were interested in the fate of the Delta series and most of them had money, influence, or both. He'd paid his dues to get control of this committee, and if everything went according to plan, three years from now he'd be sitting in the oval office rather than driving through this god-forsaken heat sink to take an uncomfortable ride up to a bunch of cramped tin cans.

The military wanted a bigger piece of the Delta series, if not the whole ball of wax. Several large corporations wanted to establish their own network of satellites and stations, free of government intervention and control. As head of the oversight committee he was in a position to nudge things in a direction that would help both viewpoints. As president, he could virtually assure it. After the committee's report, a lot of money would suddenly be available to Greer should they reach the decision he already knew they would reach. His candidacy would be well funded. He held all the cards.

He settled back into the deep cushions, let the cool air drift over him. He closed his eyes briefly, folded his hands. A forgone conclusion: Delta was a wounded bird, a sacrificial lamb. Greer could almost taste the presidency. It seemed that close.

A green eye flickered, blinked. A massive wing shifted position slightly.

Maria Rama-Diez watched them through her infrared monitors, jotting notes on a pad she balanced on her lap. The remote sensors indicated increased metabolic activity as well as a slow upswing in the complexity of neural activity. It was near the end of their darkness period and they were waking up. Maria stifled a yawn; she'd been there all night. It wasn't her shift, but when Fred had come down with a cold, she'd taken it without question. It wasn't the first time she'd pulled double duty with the mantas and it wouldn't be the last. She lived for her work and didn't think her attitude unusual at all.

On Delta III dedication to the job at hand was more the rule than the exception. It was the ultimate medical and biological research facility. Competition for the available positions was fierce; only the best or the youngest and brightest made it. Dedication was taken for granted, and among exobiologists like Maria it approached fanaticsm. Here, thanks to the *Pegasus* Project, theories were for the first time being turned into practice.

"Maria?" A whisper.

"Julia." Everybody whispered in the monitoring room. It was unnecessary, but as automatic as whispering in church or the lobby of a theatre showing a horror vid.

"How are the mantas?" Julia was a nurse and understood the mantas about as well as Maria understood a pancreas.

"Sleeping. Waking up. I've got about an hour more. What's happening today?"

"Open heart. Double valve replacement this morning. I've got to go scrub soon. Should be through in time for a late lunch or an early dinner."

"Sounds good. I'm going to collapse when my relief comes. Wake me up when you get off. Going to be busy later tonight. We're about ready to try the life island, it'll have to be checked out. I drew the lucky number, ought to be going in there within a few days."

"I'm glad for you," Julia said, resting her hand on Maria's shoulder, absently brushing her hair back, massaging the back of her neck.

fear

Maria stepped up the gain on the amplifier, rotated the camera for a better view. She touched Julia's hand.

confinement

Julia squeezed Maria's shoulder, turned and started towards the door.

protection . . . attack!

Suddenly, the male manta sprung from his perch and circled around the room, skimming the walls of their large but restrictive enclosure. His shrill, piercing cries spilled from the speaker. Julia was frozen by the door, her head twisted towards the monitor. Maria was frantically scribbling notes while shifting the camera to get it all on tape. Such activity from the usually sedate mantas was highly unusual. With a final dive, the manta descended upon the rotating camera and with a flash of talons, ripped it from the wall.

The monitor went blank. Maria sat back in her chair and realized that she'd been holding her breath.

"Devilfish," said Julia from the door. "On the coast they call mantas devilfish. In storms they surface and skim their large bodies across the tops of the waves. Once one landed on my uncle's boat. I was five and it scared me to death." She looked at the blank screen and shuddered. Her childhood was only a dream away, uncomfortably close to the surface.

"I wonder why he did that," Maria said. "We'll have to replace the camera."

In the silence her pencil slipped from her fingers. It made a hollow wooden sound as it rolled across the floor, unnoticed.

Chapter Two

═══════════════════════════════════════

Once they had lived under strange stars, felt the tug of different winds. Each in its own manner walked, crawled or flew. All they had now in common was their presence on Delta III.

Dr. Carlos Mendoza sat at his desk, flipped on the light, lifted the daily reports from the basket in front of him. His official title was Research Coordinator, Exobiology Division. He was aware that it was a purposely vague title and subject to interpretation. It could either carry a lot of responsibility or none. In his case, none. He was being phased out like last year's model and he knew why.

Exobiology was a new discipline and he had gotten in on the ground floor, but already events had passed him by. The field was growing rapidly. He was thought of as old-fashioned, out of date, conservative. He felt that he was simply cautious; that research, like all other endeavors, should proceed at a decent and orderly pace.

Even with all the advance preparation, the arrival of *Pegasus* had sent the field into a frenzy. The mission had been successful to a degree that no one had even imagined possible. No longer was exobiology a matter of playing in Earthside laboratories with a few spores and lichen painstakingly gathered from Mars and Venus. Now the science was wide open. There were many new creatures to study, many complex systems to be worked out. Yet there was a time factor, too. It looked like the *Pegasus* might have been a one-shot affair, no more were planned and funds were getting tighter all the time. The life spans of many of the organisms were unknown, they might die at any time. A few of them reproduced in captivity, others did not seem inclined to do so. The general feeling was that as much work as possible should be rushed through while the animals were still available, for there was no guarantee how long they would live. It was this rush that Carlos opposed. He felt it would lead to sloppy investigations and worthless, questionable data. It had all come to a head two weeks ago, there'd been a showdown over this and he'd lost. His replacement would be coming up soon. Until then he was just marking time, officially still on the roster, but for all practical purposes he had few duties and little authority. He was bitter about it, but there wasn't much he could do.

He spread the folders out in front of him, opened the top one.

Survey number: HSR–3476–2549–BTD. Supplement 357. Planet of Origin: Lamba Alpha XR7, IV. At-

mosphere Code: Type R3L, modified re Newrock
(see supplement 37a). Environmental Code: RD–75
with methane modification as noted, repeat cycle
36.5 hours. Gravity Sector: 0.85–g, corridor R–12,
enclosure 342. Funding: NIH/JHU/NSF, see attached for specific grant numbers. Primary investigators: Newrock, B.F. and Smith, L.C.

They called them snowballs and they lived their
lives between fire and ice. A world, a planet hung in
space, a planet of extremes; blinding heat by day and
numbing cold by night. An inhospitable world where
life had, by necessity, taken a strange turn.

Survival. Evolution. The creature had to adapt one
way or the other and somewhere, a long time ago, the
choice for its kind had been with the sun, with the
long days. It passed the nights as a frozen ball, insulated by a heavy coating of ice formed by the water
it secreted as the sun went down. Its metabolism
dropped as the temperature fell, by full darkness it
was barely alive, only the most essential biological
processes continued, and even those were at the
slowest possible pace. As the warmth of first light
reached the snowball, it stirred, unhinged its shell
and spread its folded body. Compacted by night, it
was somewhat less than a meter in diameter, but
during the peak of day it easily covered 100 square
meters like a living rug.

Extensions on its underside probed the ground for
nutrients and moisture. The form of its upper surface
was flexible, serving either to camouflage it by
blending into the background or make it stand out in
order to attract food. It was capable of extending
tendrils from its dorsal surface to collect animals that
were attracted by its color and its smell.

Asexual, the creature reproduced by budding, carrying several offspring at the same time. The one in Delta III's biosector had several buds on it already. The snowball had adjusted well.

Carlos sighed and closed the folder. The snowballs had been his pet project. He had high hopes for them. An organism that could exist and thrive under such extreme conditions should yield a lot of good information, given time and a proper investigation. Newrock and Smith were okay, but they needed guidance. Dr. Tsung-Ling was being groomed to take over the snowballs. He was a decent enough man, good credentials, but still Carlos felt a twinge of jealousy. It should have been him.

Survey number: HSR–2758–3672–NVD. Supplement 428. Planet of Origin: Beta Kappa YY5, III. Environmental Code: LW'–38, with nitrate modification, repeat cycle 26.3 hours. Gravity sector 0.93–g, corridor L–47, enclosure 123. Funding: NIH/OSU/DDI, see attached for specific grant numbers. Primary Investigators: Potts, P.A. and Blair, K.W.

Dragonfish. A stormy water world spinning in space. Life ignored the few barren land masses, evolution favored the seas, the long tidal flats. Evolution favored the strongest, the most fierce.

The dragonfish were frightful-looking omnivores, a meter and a half in length, covered with spines. Twin pairs of long feelers sprouted from the ridged crests on the top of their heads. From the front they seemed to be all teeth and mouth, from the side, all spines. In their natural environment they were fearsome eating machines, devouring almost anything that crossed their path.

In captivity, they were a problem. They weren't adjusting well at all. Although ten of them had survived transport to the orbital station, three had since died. The consensus seemed to be that there was something vital lacking from the "chicken soup" they lived in.

Since so much was unknown about these and all the other alien creatures, much of their life-support system development was educated guesswork. The scientists worked with the data collected on each specimen's home planet and added to this information by careful experimentation and observation. Much of it was detective work, deductions based on calculated assumptions for each animal. A lot of trial and error was involved and since the animals were irreplacable, the stakes were high.

The dragonfish, like finicky children, refused to eat almost everything that was placed before them, no matter how carefully prepared. Some nutrients were absorbed from their fluid environment through mesh-like filters above their mouths, but the only luck the exobiologists had achieved so far with solid food were the jellyfish. It was probably all that kept them alive.

Jellyfish weren't native to any planet, they were developed and produced on Delta III as a food substitute for some of the imported animals. Actually a very simplified animal itself, the jellyfish consisted mostly of a diffuse nervous system and connective tissue arranged in sacs that could be filled with whatever nutrients applied to the species being fed. Both the nervous system and the connective tissue were cultured from cell banks taken from Earthside sharks. There wasn't a jellyfish in its heritage at all. The outside integument could be altered to vaguely resemble the natural food source for most of the animals.

The dragonfish ate them, but even so, they didn't look like they were getting along too well. Autopsies on the three that had died yielded ambiguous information open to conflicting interpretations. Some said the animals were starving, others said there was something toxic either in the chicken soup or the jellyfish. A thorough analysis of the problem was underway, involving several people on board, thousands more on Earth, and a tremendous amount of computer time.

Carlos made a notation in the margin of the form. It would probably be ignored, he thought. When he got back to Earth, he figured things would be different. He'd be an authority there. An exobiologist with experience could always find a good position. Still he was jealous, angry. They were wrong, all of them.

One of the people involved with the dragonfish was Maria Rama-Diez, another was Rob McGreggor. Maria was involved because she was an upper level exobiologist who went from species to species rather than being assigned, as most were, to one particular animal. Rob was involved simply because he was a parasitologist with a broad, nonrestrictive background. Also because he was curious.

A really thorough examination meant that the dead dragonfish had to be examined for parasites as one of the almost limitless number of possible causes for their death. It was a nearly hopeless task. Very little was known about any of the animals and nothing whatsoever about any possible systems of parasites or commensals they might have. Since it was a hopeless case, Rob was unavoidably attracted to it.

Rob was working under the low power of his dissecting microscope, moving small sections of dragonfish digestive system around in a shallow dish. He had no idea what he was looking for, but he hoped he'd recognize it when, and if, he saw it. It would probably show up as something unusual, but that didn't help too much. Everything about these animals was unusual. Alien environmental pathways had taken these creatures in truly novel directions. Even their approach to such a seemingly straight-forward and universal activity as digestion had taken a strange turn.

Instead of the finger-like villi so common in terrestrial systems, the dragonfish had a large digestive sac packed full of interlocking, hairlike filiments that served as a filter of sorts. Each filiment was covered with thousands of small buds that, when touched, sent out sharp-pointed tentacles. The tentacles thrashed around, apparently breaking down the food particles. The sharp points contained a powerful digestive enzyme. It was a complicated system, but, in reality, not much more complex than the churning tubes inside his own body. It was just that somewhere in the murky past of a strange planet evolution had taken a different path.

The buzzer rang. Pushing back his chair, Rob turned to the counter where he was staining his latest series of slides. He removed the rack from a dish of brightly colored solution, drained it over a small towel, and dropped it into the next solution, resetting the timer for ten minutes. The door opened. It was Maria.

"Hard at work, I see."

"Serial sections," answered Bob, setting the timer back on the counter. "Air sac tissue from the second dragonfish."

"Any leads?"

"Not really. Just thought I'd take a look."

"Might as well check for surface obstructions while you're at it. Carlos suspects a metabolic breakdown, but it could be much simpler. He tends to look for the most complicated answers to any problem."

"I don't know about Carlos, but *I'm* in way over my head. The deeper I get into this, the more confused I get. My schistosomes look like simple one-celled animals compared to this mess."

"We're all in over our heads, Rob. That's why we're getting so much good information. All this is new to everybody. It's just that your background is different from ours. We're trained to expect to be confused all the time, while you try to make sense out of everything. You bring a different approach to the problem, that's why I asked you to help."

"I don't seem to be helping much."

"You're doing fine. Something will turn up." She turned towards the door, paused. "I'm taking the life island into the manta's enclosure later today. Expect I'll be tied up with them for the next couple of days. If you come up with anything, let Carlos know."

Rob groaned and Maria broke into a quick smile.

"If Carlos doesn't seem to be listening, just leave a note for me in my lab. I'll be in and out a lot. Oh, by the way, you can have Jodie back this afternoon. We borrowed her for some work on the snowballs this morning.

"Thanks," said Rob. "I can use her. Good luck with the mantas. Bring me back a butterfly to play with."

"I've been looking forward to this for a long time. It'll be fun." She closed the door quietly behind her.

Rob's timer rang and he moved the slides to the next bath.

Senator Arnold Greer was uncomfortable and cramped. There wasn't anything he could do about it. He didn't like situations he couldn't control. The Earth hung just above his left elbow, the stars were bright points of light.

Delta II would probably be just like Delta I, the station he was pulling soundlessly away from. They were both mainly manufacturing stations; alloys, precision equipment, crystals, and the like. He had no real quarrel with them, only the fact that they were under government control. It was true that private companies and other nations could contract to do work on the stations, but there were too many rules and regulations. Regulations stifled private industry, kept it from growing in its own direction.

With any luck, he'd be able to get Delta II out of the way quickly. Couldn't be all that much there, anyway. Just a lot of scientists and engineers afraid of losing their jobs, nervously demonstrating their specialties. Greer swore that if he had to sit through one more "perfect ball bearing" being cast, he'd throw up, zero-g or not.

Delta III would take longer. All those crazy animals were pretty popular on Earth, even if it did

cost an arm and a leg to bring them here. And he'd
have to be careful on the medical part—nobody
knocked open heart surgery. The research part was
the most vulnerable. Millions of dollars being tossed
down the drain to find out the sex habits of blah,
blah, blah. It would all come into shape.

The pilot and co-pilot moved in front of him,
talking to themselves. The craft was too small, not
enough room in back. Greer's mind wandered.
Maybe there was something on the captain on Delta
III. If there was, Hickson would have it. He turned
to speak to his secretary, sitting in the seat beside
him. Hickson was asleep, floating just above his seat,
kept in place by the loose straps. Asleep. How could
anyone sleep cooped up like this? Damn him,
anyway.

Maria stood in the sterile ready room outside the
airlock to the manta's enclosure. A white-suited
medical team was attaching leads to various parts of
her body. Tight-lipped technicians swarmed over the
life island, triple checking everything, working with a
single-minded determination, more like ants than
people. It amused Maria that they seemed so grim.
Although she took her work seriously, there was
always room for a joke or wisecrack, a laugh to put
things in perspective. This crew didn't relax at all until they were off duty. Then, she knew, they really
swung loose. A couple of them had made passes at
her. But the minute they got a wrench or a piece of
test equipment in their hands, it was all business. She
realized abstractly that her life was in their hands,
but the excitement of the project so far over-
shadowed the dangers that they seldom crossed her
mind.

The empty life island had been placed inside the manta's enclosure for the last two days so that the animals could become accustomed to its presence. After a few initial inspections, they had pretty much ignored it. Now it was being readied for its first working trip inside.

The life support island looked even bulkier than the early space suit prototypes. It looked like a robot gone wild, a small nightmare tank. It was efficient as all hell.

Maria climbed in. It was a tight fit and she had to go through all sorts of awkward contortions to connect the wires that hung from her body. It took several minutes to get herself all hooked up.

She half stood, half sat on a small swivel platform inside the LSI, her head sticking up into the bubble of one-way glass on top. At her fingertips were controls for the numerous special purpose extensions that hung on the side of the island like prosthetic arms. A thin rod adjusted direction of movement and speed. The LSI could move in any direction at once, but could only do so in two speeds: slow and slower. It just wasn't built for rapid transit. There were three LSIs on Delta III, the other two were only used outside the station and were appropriately modified. Maria switched to internal support as the crew fastened her in.

It would be possible for a person to live for over a week inside the LSI, but today's schedule called for only an hour or two inside the enclosure. Primarily, Maria was going in to collect butterflies.

The butterflies, of course, weren't butterflies at all. About the size of the palm of your hand, the butterflies had round bodies, slightly concave, like a suction cup. Their three pairs of wings were large and laced with brightly colored veins. Captured along with the mantas as a kind of an extra bonus, they had a complex, and as yet not fully understood, relationship with the mantas. It was assumed that they were either symbionts or commensals, since they didn't seem to injure the mantas. They were also very prolific and short lived. The adults laid a pair of eggs in the gill folds of the male mantas, and promptly died. Always the *male* manta and they always died. The eggs hatched in a matter of hours, releasing a wingless larvae that apparently did not feed. *How did it develop so fast? Did it have stored food? How or what did it metabolize?* It dropped off the manta in a short time, and sought out a dark place where it spun a crystalline cocoon. After two or three days, the adult butterfly would hatch from the cocoon and, after a few minutes fluffing and drying its wings, fly away. It seemed to attach itself to almost any solid surface, showing only a slight preference for the mantas. The adults would live about a week before they laid their eggs and died. How they fed or what they ate was a subject of controversy. They, like all the alien species on Delta III, held more mysteries than answers. Within the myriad mysteries these creatures held were clues to questions about life on other planets as well as insights on the uniqueness of life on earth. Perhaps answers to some of Earth's pressing problems could be found by examining these representatives of far away worlds. For a thousand different reasons, people were curious about the alien creatures.

Maria more than most.

She slipped on the headphones and tongued the intercom open. She had a slight cramp in her left leg.

"Let's get this show on the road," she said, anxious to get started.

"About five more minutes, Ms. Rama-Diez. We're calibrating the monitor pack now." That was Robert Wells, handling communication with the LSI this shift. He was one of the men who had previously made a pass at her. His voice was as flat and emotionless as mission control. All business. She cconsidered cracking a joke on him, but he was too serious for that. She'd tried it before and failed. None of them seemed to have any sense of humor at all. Not on duty, at least.

Maria had been born in a small village on the Yucatan peninsula and was only thirteen when she graduated from the *Universidad de Coahuila* in Saltillo. By that time she had collected, identified, and catalogued over twenty species of small animals and insects. She was a voracious reader and one of those rare people who could pick up obscure information from one branch of scientific discipline and immediately see implications in another branch, no matter how far removed. It was that talent that brought her to the newly developed exobiology program at Cocoa Beach, in the shadow of the space program. It was that talent which, five years later, took her up to Delta III.

The last amber light turned green. "Ready, Ms. Rama-Diez."

"Roger. I'm heading for the entrance chamber." She twisted the rod, started moving. "By the way, Robert, you can call me Maria."

"Roger, Ms. . . . er, Maria." Almost got him that time.

While she waited inside the chamber for the outside air to be vented and the manta's atmosphere pumped in, she practiced flexing some of the various appendages she'd be using. On the small screen to the left of her steering rod she could see herself being monitored. Everything seemed to be working okay. She made an obscene gesture with one of the appendages. A muted chuckle came through her headphones. Maybe they had a buried sense of humor after all.

"We're starting to open the inner lock door."

"Got you, Robert, I'm ready."

The door opened and Maria slowly rolled into the enclosure. Her pulse was up: 120 beats per minute. Her respiration rate was up: 40 breaths per minute. She was excited.

An eyelid slid back and dreams of mountains and high winds fell away. *Movement.* He tensed, crouched down on his perch and unfolded his wings in preparation for flight. *Danger?* It moved slowly, like before. But, unlike before, it didn't stop. He glanced at his mate. Sleeping. He squawked, she woke. *Wrongness.* He pushed into flight and circled her.

Confinement. He felt closed in. There was no place to fly, no place to escape. In the mountains there were many places to go, thermals to climb. Escape from any danger was only a matter of beating his powerful wings. Beyond the mountains were other mountains, other valleys. The sky was limitless and it belonged to him and his kind. Now there were walls, barriers, things he had never known before. And the new strong feelings, the instinct to reproduce the species, had come upon him and it was perhaps the strongest urge he had ever felt. It ran through every fiber of his body. All he could do was protect his mate and he would protect her till his death.

He flew a tight pattern around his wary mate and kept his eyes on the strange intruder.

Maria allowed herself a moment of fantasy. In her mind the walls blurred as she concentrated on the mantas. She imagined herself on their home planet, a planet she had no hope of ever setting foot on. This was as close as she could ever be, but in her mind she felt the searing sun, the warm breezes. She stood on the sand and watched the majestic beasts above.

Somewhere in her professional mind were the butterflies, the protocol for collecting them, the number to be gathered, the methods of tagging them and a thousand other details. But she was only conscious of being so close to an alien species, closer than she'd ever been before. She could feel herself blending into their world. She knew that it was poor behavior for an exobiologist, but her feelings were so overwhelming that they involved her totally.

Her involvement was so deep that she didn't see the light flash from green to amber. A tenth of a second later it flashed to red. She didn't see that either. Her eyes had filmed over by that time.

Something sharp burned her lungs. She clawed at her throat as everything whirled around her. Her forehead banged the rim of the bubble as she fell in a slump against the wall of the LSI.

All she heard was Robert's voice, tinny and distant in her headphones. "Damn," he said softly. There was emotion in his voice.

Actually, Robert was too busy to say much of anything else. At the first flash of amber he had hit the override switch and toggeled it over to the backup

system. Even at that, it hadn't been quick enough.
The light burned red, red as death. "Damn," he said.
Immediately he switched the LSI to remote control
and started it back towards the lock.

"We've got a shunt on our hands," he said to the
crew. "Looks like a total. Get that chamber ready
fast." A klaxon bell ringing in his ear startled him. It
was a second or two before he realized it was the
medicalert for this sector and that he had set it in
motion by automatically pushing a button. He
honestly didn't remember doing it.

The medic team was there before they got Maria
out of the chamber.

The captain's living quarters connected directly
with the board room so Riggs was there in a matter of
seconds after the first alarm. Technically his presence
wasn't required, but as a matter of policy he followed
everything as closely as possible. Most of the crew
felt that he watched things too closely. He knew what
everybody thought: *busybody*. He also knew that a
good commander kept track of what was going on,
had to be on top of everything. He looked over
Brown's shoulder.

Malfunction in Life Support Island #2, currently
located in biosector Baker, 0.5–g level. The mantas.
The person who had been using the island inside the
manta's enclosure was Maria Rama-Diez, age 32,
exobiologist. Valve LSI2–25/86/7C had stuck in the
open position, causing a shunt in the island's air flow
system. For the eighteen seconds it took to correct
the situation she had been exposed to the manta's atmosphere. She was alive. The medics were with her.
It didn't look too bad.

The island would be out of commission for quite some time. It would have to be repaired, completely checked out again. So would Maria Rama-Diez.

Even at that she had been lucky. The mantas were basically carbo/oxy creatures and their atmosphere, though caustic, was tolerable in very small doses. Maria had, according to the initial examination, suffered some minor lung damage, injury to her mucous membranes, and partial eye involvement. All easily repairable. She would be quarantined for the mandatory period of time, poked and prodded by assorted doctors who specialized in poking and prodding, then sent back to work. The situation was under control. Robert Wells had been right on top of it, done everything possible. Brown had handled this end well, as expected.

Riggs stood silently for the remaining fifteen minutes of Brown's shift. He sat in his chair at the precise time, activated it. Rituals were performed, the mantle of immediate responsibility shifted. Brown headed out the door. He needed a drink and he knew where he could find one. That had been close.

Riggs relaxed, feeling the flow of the board. Too bad for—what was her name? Julia. Julia Carroll, female, age 36, coronary care nurse, team 2. Maria's lover. He smiled. Perhaps he did follow things a little too closely.

Slipping into the rhythm of his shift, Riggs absently tapped the controls to allocate more hot water to the women's one-g washroom.

The male manta circled. He watched the strange figure enter, pause, disappear. For ten minutes he

hung in the air, waiting. Nothing happened so he settled back on his perch. Apparently the danger had
passed.

It was hours before he would allow himself to
sleep. During that time he methodically scanned the
enclosure for movement. He saw only walls, but in
his mind there were mountains and storms.

Chapter Three

Rob turned off his microscope, leaned back and rubbed his eyes. Long day. His back hurt.

It was frustrating, his work was moving very slowly. Most of the research on the dragonfish had stopped when Maria had her accident and Rob had gone back to concentrating on his schistosome problem. He carefully filed away the slides he'd been working on. The creatures were more adaptable than anyone had thought. Somewhere there must be an answer, but so far everything led up blind alleys. He had gathered some useful information, if nothing earthshaking or startling, to justify the time and expense. Still, something might come of it yet. He adjusted the airflow on one of the aquariums holding his snails.

Rob had infected these particular snails about six weeks ago, so they should be about ready. Wearing gloves and using forceps, he placed a half dozen of them in a small container. Later he would collect the infective larvae as the snails shed them.

He planned to infect some sterile-raised mice with this batch. Sterile environments were easy to come by on Delta III. This particular group of mice, a C-5/RD strain, were in their fifth generation under these conditions. It was possible that they might react differently to the parasite than regular mice. Maybe their immunological system was different due to their having been raised in a sterile environment. It was worth a try. Rob didn't know what to expect. Neither did his ground-based advisor. Edward Lyle. If they knew the answers, they wouldn't have to perform the experiments. Rob put the lid on the container of snails. He swabbed his hands and arms with alcohol and closed up shop for awhile.

Maria lowered herself gently into the offered chair.

"You okay?" asked Linda.

"I guess so. Still a little weak." Eyes downcast, she picked at some imaginary lint on her slacks. "Got a minute?"

"Sure," said Linda, moving some forms to the side of her desk. "What's the problem?"

"It's probably nothing, but . . . uh, can this be off the record?"

"Why?" Linda looked up sharply.

"I don't want to be taken off this project. I just can't. This is my life, my whole life. Since I was a child I've wanted to do this kind of work. I don't want to lose it. But I've got to talk to someone. You're a friend. You're the only one I felt I could trust."

Linda leaned back in her chair. "I won't take notes, if that's what you mean. I'm required to report anything I come across that might interfere with the operations up here, but if we can take care of it ourselves, it won't go any further. Remember, I'm only a clinical psychologist, not a psychiatrist, if your problem is of that nature."

"I'm not sure what it's about at all," said Maria. "It all started soon after the accident. I mean, the dreams started. Long dreams, extremely vivid, nearly always the same. Flying mantas, always the same pair we have here, I don't know how I know that in my dream, but I do. They're not caged up, either. I dream of their world, their mountains, their rivers. Somehow it is all superimposed over the countryside near where I grew up. It's all jumbled together. In my dream I'm standing there watching them and I can't move. I'm naked and helpless. Somehow I get the impression that they need help and I can't do anything. My mother calls to me, I can't answer her. The mantas squawk and I am frozen like a statue." She paused.

"Go on," said Linda.

"That's all," said Maria abruptly. She tensed in her chair.

"No," said Linda. "That's not all. I can't help you if you don't tell me everything."

"I am!" It came too loud. It came too quick.

"Come on, Maria. I know you better than that. You're an easy-going person and a lousy liar. If the dream was all that was bothering you, it would be more in character for you to tell me about it and laugh it off, make a joke about it. What's the rest of the story?"

"Okay. I might as well get it out. The dream, well, it doesn't only come at night. Lately I have been kind of daydreaming or something. I'll drift off and suddenly I'll be aware of the dream and I'll snap out of it. It only lasts a few seconds. It couldn't be anything, could it?''

"I don't know," said Linda, reaching for a pad and pen. She scribbled something on the pad, tore off the top sheet and handed it to Maria. "Take this to Candy. I want her to run an EEG on you, just to be on the safe side. I'll have her send the interpretation directly to me. It's probably nothing, but I'll want to check it." She settled back, tapping the pen against a fingernail on her left hand.

"You don't think there's something wrong with my brain, do you?''

"No, not really. But we ought to rule it out, anyway. I think you went back to work too soon, that's all," said Linda. "And I think maybe you're too close to all this, particularly to the mantas. Sounds like you're identifying with them."

"No!"

"It could—"

"That's just not possible. I'm an exobiologist, a scientist. I'm trained to be objective. My dreams have nothing to do with my functioning on the project, nothing at all. I won't let you say that they do."

"Come on, Maria, calm down. You need some rest. You went back to work too soon and you've been working too hard. Why don't you take some time off? Carlos can handle things for awhile."

"Carlos can't handle anything, certainly not what we're doing now. It would take days to bring him up to date and even then, well, Carlos isn't very imaginative."

Linda laughed. "He is pretty stodgy, isn't he?"

"Yes," Maria said with a grin, relaxing. "A bit

too somber and plodding for my tastes. He'll be leaving soon anyway." She straightened her slacks, stood up. "You're right, I guess. I'll try to cut back a little. Get some more rest."

"Don't forget to see Candy."

"I won't," said Maria, heading for the door. "Thanks for your time."

"Take care," said Linda.

Outside the door, Maria slumped against the wall. Why hadn't she come out with it all? Why couldn't she tell Linda about the time she blanked out for over an hour while monitoring the mantas? Or the experiment she nearly ruined because she forgot a crucial step? Or the thousand other things she had forgotten or done wrong and somehow managed to cover up? She wasn't much different from the mantas, after all. Survival and preservation were strong driving forces. If she lost this position, there would never be another. She'd be finished. She crumpled the slip of paper in her hand into a small ball and dropped it down the recycler. Maybe next week.

Linda closed Maria's folder. She'd made some coded notations on the back of one of the forms. It didn't look good. She'd hate to recommend that Maria be sent back down, but it looked like she might have to do it. But again, it *could* be fatigue. She'd give it the benefit of a doubt for now. Surely Maria would know before she got into real trouble. She made a note to see Maria in a week and to check with Candy in the morning.

She refiled Maria's folder and pulled the papers she'd been working on back to the center of the desk. They were the final breakdowns of the post-tour psychological profiles for the crew members leaving this afternoon. She looked at the digital on the wall. The shuttle would be arriving in another twenty minutes and the crew would be leaving within three hours. She didn't like it.

There wasn't anything specific she could put her finger on, but something was just a little wrong. Individually the profiles looked okay, within expected limits. Looking at them as a group, however, things didn't come out as well. An unusually high percentage of them showed many of the symptoms of fatigue; cabin fever, perhaps. A large number exhibited high anxiety levels, tendencies towards quick irritability. There were conflicts and friction between several individuals. This was primarily a maintenance crew on a relatively short stay. Their unions required that they spend no more than six weeks aboard the station without a rotation to Earth. By and large, they were usually a little more unstable than the regular crew, but this seemed more than normal. Their efficiency had fallen off in the last week and a half, too. Four of them would miss the shuttle today because they were in sick bay. That was too many. Maybe it was just a bad bunch, a statistical fluke. Maybe. She'd run this batch through again and see Dr. Turner about it.

Something was bothering her, but the closer she tried to look at the problem, the more its edges blurred and she became confused by the bulk of data. She rubbed her eyes. It didn't help.

The small spacecraft carrying Senator Greer from Delta II arrived at the same time as the shuttle from Earth. There was a momentary delay as they jockeyed for position prior to docking. Greer hated delays, especially while cooped up in these small ships. He wished he could just hop on the shuttle and go back down with it. Well, it shouldn't take too long. Dinner with the captain, a couple of tours, some demonstrations, a few meetings. It shouldn't take more than a couple days. Three at most.

The shuttle took the primary docking site, relegating them to the smaller dock. Greer felt as if he was being forced to use the servants' entrance. Even getting out of the small ship was complicated. Everything seemed to be part of a great conspiracy to make his life more difficult. By the time he finally got on board Delta III he was in a foul mood. Meeting Riggs didn't improve things at all.

Rob had reached the cafeteria before he realized it was too early to meet Linda. She wouldn't get off for at least another hour. They were lucky she would be getting off at all. In addition to her duties as a psychologist, she had been pressed into duty assisting the medical staff. They were shorthanded these days. Something seemed to be going around. Linda didn't get much free time.

They had never really had very much free time. Books and exams seemed to be constant obstacles between them. The times they'd managed to steal, they had put to good use. Once there was a whole summer. Lazy days on the beach and moonlight walks. It had been nice. Very nice. Someday, maybe again.

The cafeteria was loud and crowded, so Rob decided to walk over and watch the mantas to kill the hour. The 0.5-g would feel restful after a day hunched over his microscope.

The female manta was gravid and about to give birth. There was wide speculation, accompanied by numerous wagers, as to the date of delivery. Even the exobiologists had joined the pool and their bets were spread out as far as the rest.

A half dozen people were sitting around watching. The female manta hung by her long talons from the supports like a giant bat, wings spread wide. The male made occasional passes at her, coasting on the breeze generated by several large fans set in the ends of their enclosure.

Rob sat next to Ed Brown. Unlike Riggs or Gonzales, Brown tended to mix socially with the crew. This was his third tour on Delta III. Previously he had been commander on one of the Gamma stations. They had been phased out with the construction of the Delta series of satellites, many of their parts cannibalized for reuse in the fourth generation stations. What was left of them still hung in orbit. They would stay in orbit for hundreds of years, expensive junk. Brown and Rob had gotten to know each other fairly well. They occasionally indulged in games of chance together, usually in the form of fierce poker games, much to Rob's misfortune.

The female manta had several small gashes in her belly. The exobiologists said this was normal. The infant manta actually clawed its way out of the mother, using its talons. The male secreted some sort of a fine mist as it flew around the female. The mist accelerated her clotting time so that she wouldn't bleed to death. Being used to the strange and complex life cycles of parasites, Rob thought it was ingenious, an alien adaptation. Ed thought it was gross and disgusting.

"They look like fish out of water," said Brown.

"Um," said Rob, distracted. He was trying to reconcile the image of the caged animals with his thoughts of their world of wind, their lives before capture. Something he had once read, a poem about bats by a man called Randall Jarrell, skipped through his mind and was gone.

"Play some cards?" asked Brown. "There's a hot game going on in Engineering."

"I don't know." Something on his mind, elusive. Bats? Mantas? It slipped away.

"Sam's there. Tony'll be there too." Tony had lots of money and a weakness for drawing to inside straights.

"Yeah, I guess so," said Rob, standing. "Can't let the rest of those jokers take all his money."

The engineering deck was stark and functional compared to the rest of the station. Not that there were a lot of frills on Delta III, but somewhere along the line the psychologists had recommended that such niceties as walls and floors might keep the crew in a better frame of mind. Here there were no walls, only exposed conduits and coils of multicolored wires. The floors were open metal grillwork, hinged to allow easy access to the complicated plumbing visible beneath. The entire area was ringed with gauges and valves, meters and flashing lights. A huge console was built into one corner. It was covered with complicated dials and computer displays. A ham sandwich with two bites out of it lay on the console. So did a pair of feet. The sandwich and feet belonged to Sam and he removed them both at the same time.

"Just in time, boys," said Sam. "I was about to go off shift and partake of a small game of cards. Hey, Bert!" He motioned to one of the men standing around. "Take over here, will you? I got a little business to take care of."

An alcove off the main deck held sleeping and recreation quarters for the engineering crew. Like the doctors and nurses, they slept near their patients. Unlike the doctors, the arteries they tended were composed of metal, not flesh, and the heartbeats they monitored were those of a station spinning in space. They tended to be a rough and tumble group. Sam was rough and he'd been known to tumble a bit, but he was the best. Not a man this side of Mars knew machinery better than he did.

Three men were sitting at a table, warming up a deck of cards. They exchanged mumbled greetings all around. Coins, bills, and the credit slips used for cash on the station appeared in small piles in front of each player.

The cards were cut and spread out in the middle of the table. Each player took one, high card dealt and named the game. It was a routine they had been through many times before. Their actions were a ritual that had been standardized long before any of them had been born. Like Mississippi gamblers they settled back and tried to look cool and detached. They didn't know the significance of aces and eights and probably weren't too sure who Doc Holliday had been, but they played their roles to perfection. They could have been seated around a green felt table at the Last Chance Saloon.

The poker games were a regular feature of life on Delta III, and had been since the station was constructed. Sam was one of the few who had been there from the beginning and one of the first things he had done was grab three other players for a game of cutthroat. He had used up most of his personal weight allotment bringing up sealed decks of Bicycle playing cards. There were also a few overweight charges against Engineering that the brass chose to ignore. Playing cards never appeared on the manifests, but somehow there always seemed to be a fresh deck available.

The rules were simple and well established by now: quarter ante, pot limit, and no games with wild cards. They took their playing seriously. A lot of money changed hands, but usually between the same people. It all worked out about even in the long run. There wasn't much else to do with money on the station, anyway.

Rob drew a queen. "Five card stud," he said, raking the cards towards him. It looked like it could turn out to be a good afternoon. Tony was seated to his right. It crossed his mind that he should be doing something else, but for the life of him, he couldn't remember what it was.

Julia stood to the left of Dr. Lennox, a tray of stainless steel instruments between them. The lights overhead were glaringly bright and her upper lip, under the blue mask, had a thin layer of sweat.

There were eleven people in the basic surgical team. Three stood at each side of the patient, two each at his head and feet, one rotated around the circle, helping wherever needed. They worked, as always, with a minimum of conversation. It was a team effort and each individual knew his job well. Julia reached out over the sterile drape and adjusted a hemostat. Without looking up, Dr. Lennox nodded. The patient's chest was split open, his exposed heart beat rhythmically. They were approaching a critical stage in the operation, a mitral valve replacement. A difficult but routine procedure. Routine, that is, on Delta III.

Twenty years ago, on Earth, he wouldn't have had a chance.

PATIENT NOTES

Name: Times, David R.

Age: 48

Residence: Complex 37, Level 5, Wash D.C.

Occupation: Shipping Clerk

Marital Status: Married. 29 years.

Children: Two. Female. Age 20 & 23.

Uni-Med Number: 28B–3013–52L.

Home Med Bank: DC/SW/47

Personal Physician: Dr. James Moore

Blood Type: O Neg.

Allergies: None

Diagnosis: Chronic heart disease, degenerative mitral valve.

Recommendation: Low-grav surgery & recovery

Prognosis: Good

The prognosis was good because of the lessened stress of low gravity surgery performed with the best of equipment on Delta III. Good because he could recover where gravity didn't pull at his damaged heart, where his body could adjust slowly for his return to Earth. Good because his replacement valve was made of an absolutely smooth alloy that could only be manufactured in space; one that didn't, unlike even the best Earth-made valves, cause blood to clot on its surface. On Earth he would have been dead in a year. Thanks to Delta III, he could expect another 48 years of life.

The anesthesiologist, sitting at the head of the patient, made a small adjustment, looked up at the boards to check the results.

The boards were raised CRT screens connected to two complicated and sophisticated machines. Candy, the EEG tech, sat in front of one. John, one of the chemistry techs, sat at the other.

The machine that Candy ran was a more complex version of the one that she used to measure brain waves in her office. It was a 24-channel unit, with 16 channels giving a continuous EEG readout. Another three channels gave an EKG reading, while others measured respiration, skin potential, rectal temperature and arterial and venous blood pressure.

John's machine was, in essence, a compact chemistry laboratory. It displayed continual readings of acetone, ammonia, amylase, bilirubin, B.U.N., calcium, cholesterol, creatine, sodium, potassium, chlorides, glucose, SGOT, CPK and SGPT. Every five minutes it popped up a fibrinogen and PPT. In addition, it monitored pH of the blood along with the pO_2 and pCO_2, automatically calculating the acid/base balance.

The readouts from both machines were not only used during the operation, but were stored on tape so that they could be recovered to provide a clinical picture of the operation as well as being used for research.

"Pump?" asked Dr. Lennox.

"Primed," said one of the technicians at the patient's head. "One point five liters Lactated Ringers."

"Arterial connection secure," said one of the nurses, lightly touching a catheter that ran from the pump into an incision at the patient's groin.

"Venous connection secure." Another nurse, across from Julia, touched a catheter that exited from the vicinity of the patient's collarbone.

"Start pump," said Dr. Lennox.

"*Mark,*" said the team leader, starting a clock into motion.

Linda left Dr. Turner's office with a vague feeling of dissatisfaction. The crew had rotated back to Earth and neither she nor Dr. Turner had been able to find anything to substantiate her misgivings about their psychological profiles. Dr. Turner had promised to have one of the boys run it through the computer as soon as there was time, but neither one of them had much hope that anything would come of it. It was probably just a fluke. She decided to go by the nursing station on her way to the cafeteria to meet Rob.

The nursing station was a mess. Intensive care was getting ready to receive a patient from the OR, a heart operation where something had gone wrong. A Code Three Red had been called in Stores, where a large crate being unloaded from the last shuttle had pinned two men down. Already shorthanded, several people had been called off the floor to respond to the code.

"You look like you could use some help," said Linda to Susan, the floor supervisor.

"That's an understatement," said Susan, shaking her head. "Our relief is coming in a half hour early and I've got everyone in who was on call, but we're still short. Everything would happen today—I've got six nurses on sick call."

"Let me watch the desk for you," offered Linda.

"Thanks, that would help a lot. I really should be down there with the code. It looks bad. Shouldn't have happened." She picked a tray from the rack by the crash cart. "Somebody made a big mistake."

"Anything special I should watch out for?"

"Keep an eye on the monitor for bed five. That's Mrs. Garson and she's pretty unstable. I've got Mabel over there now, but this is her first week in the unit. Ordinarily I wouldn't have her by herself so soon, but . . . you know how it is."

Linda nodded. "Want me to come in tonight? I'm free."

"You're a doll, Linda. Just pencil yourself in anywhere you want. Got to run. Thanks."

Linda enjoyed working in the nursing area and she volunteered whenever they were short. She was an RN herself and had left a good position to return to school for her training and Ph.D. in psychology. It hadn't been an easy decision at the time. Although she was happy with the way her career had progressed and developed, she still missed the day to day details of nursing. She kept her license current, took the required exam every 24 months. Lately it had come in handy.

Things settled down after a short time. One of the men from Stores went to the OR, the other was treated at the scene and brought back to the unit. He'd be okay. Susan came back and Linda went to the cafeteria to meet Rob.

Although she was late, Rob wasn't there. She got a cup of coffee from the machine and sat down to wait. Dr. Faraday came by and made a crude pass at her. Annoyed, she snapped at him. The coffee was bitter and cold. Rob was late. Where was he? She had work to do. There were too many people in the cafeteria, they made too much noise. It was hot, she felt dizzy. Opening a folder, she tried again to make sense out of the post-tour tests. She only became more confused. Another cup of cold coffee didn't help. She remembered she'd signed up to work in the unit later in the evening. Maybe she'd better take a nap first. A nap sounded like a good idea. Can't wait for Rob forever. Where was he? It occurred to her that she ought to be mad and she was. She was still mad when she got back to her cubicle, but by the time that she fell asleep, she'd forgotten what it was that she was supposed to be mad about.

Maria walked slowly down the corridor. She felt like she was floating, disconnecting from the things around her. It was as though she existed on two levels. On one level, the far lower one, she imagined, she talked to people she met in the corridor, made appropriate responses to their greetings, their questions. But on the other level, the *real* level, she was free. Free as she had never known before. Her mind wandered between planets, spanned the galaxy. Here more than any place else. Here in the corridor, not just *any* corridor, but this special one. Here among friends, among doorways to other worlds. She stopped walking, pressed her face against the cool, tempered glass. Her left hand absently caressed a line of rivets at a joint in the wall. A few feet beyond, separated by glass and steel, the snowball was unfolding. For Maria, the walls disappeared.

She was one with the snowball. Its movements were her movements, its feelings were her own. Time shifted, she could feel her metabolism slow.

Daylight. Relief from the frozen night. The dark cold endured, another day to be faced. Survival was food, warmth. Slowly it/she seeked out the sun. Like a seed pod, the shell of ice cracked and fell away. With great care the folds inched outwards. Ah, there, heat! More. More. Unfolding, reaching, stretching.

*My God, feel it. Like standing naked on a rock above
the ocean in the last flash/flush of childhood with all
the suns of yesterday warming your body. Like the
first day at the beach after the coldest winter in years.
Mother, where are you? The blanket is spread.
Where are you? So warm. Food waits. Life begins.*

The copper-based blood, stored in great pools deep
inside the snowball for the frigid night, streams outwards toward the extremities. Vessels pulse, expand,
contract. The hearts beat quicker. Respiratory slits
open and close. Overhead a strange sun glows. The
walls are gone. The barren horizon stretches forever.
Snug against the ground, the flattened body extends
still further. Eyespots dilate, vision from a hundred
inputs, somehow integrated into one comprehensive
image. *Like being a hundred people. Like being one
person a hundred times.* The probes sneak down
from its/hers/our/my belly, working through small
cracks, pushing dirt and pebbles out of the way.
Cold. The planet's surface is still cold. Like digging
in frozen sand. Small chips of ice melt on the probe's
surface, are quickly absorbed, pumped to reservoirs,
nutrients filtered, extracted, metabolized, water integrated into the system. No waste. An arid planet.
Nothing must be wasted. Around the larger rocks. A
thousand probes, a thousand fingers from its/our
belly digging, moving, digging, We move. We feel.
We live. The strange sun is higher in the sky, chasing
a phantom moon grown dim. The air warms. Heat,
oh, feel the heat. Small creatures start to move
through the air. It is time. We extend out tendrils
from our upper surface. *How beautiful they are.*
They unfold like small flowers. From glands we
secrete a sticky, smelly fluid. The fluid is pumped
through the tendrils to the buds on the end. Small

creatures are attracted, caught in the sticky fluid. The
tendrils retract, bringing the creature, bringing food.
A mouth opens up at the base of the tendril. The
creature is chewed by rows of chitenous teeth. It is
crunchy, there is no sense of taste. The creature is
broken down to its component parts, metabolized,
becomes energy. This pattern is repeated by hundreds
of tendrils. The day is hot now, the sun is high in the
sky.

"Maria?"

We move, constantly move. Quicker now that our
body is full of energy. We are one with the ground,
the air. We draw energy and strength from the sun,
the water, the small creatures, a thousand sources.
We undulate out of the sheer happiness of being alive
another day. We probe the dirt, reach for the sky.
There are no limits. *It feels so good.* So warm, the
sun. So warm.

"Are you all right, Maria?"

All right? Of course. It is beautiful, this oneness
with our surroundings. It gives, we take, we work
together, we live, we survive. A cold hand on my
forehead.

Forehead? Hand? Coldness?

"Maria!"

No. Let me be. It's going, shifting. I'm losing it.
The walls, the glass. No. Gone the sun. The probes,
the tendrils, the warmth. A cold hand. The oneness,
the closeness. Going, going. *No.*

"No!"

"Maria. What's wrong?" It was Jodie.

There it goes. Fainter now. Gone. Gone. Was it
ever there?

Maria turned from the glass, faced Jodie. "I'm

fine, thanks," she said, but her hands were trembling.

"Are you sure? You don't look too good."

"I was resting. A little tired." She leaned against the wall.

"Is there anything I can do to help? Get you something?"

"No," said Maria. The wall was cool.

"I'm fine," she lied.

One thing Greer was good at was digging out the dirt. He had a positive talent for that, had made good use of it over the years. If there was anything wrong he could sniff it out in a minute. Even if there was nothing wrong, he could usually find something to bend to fit his needs.

"I understand you're being fired, Dr. Mendoza," said Greer. He sat in the suite that had been provided for him. It was the largest one on the station, seldom used. Still it was too small for him.

"Not fired, exactly, Senator . . . " Carlos looked uncomfortable. Greer could do that to people.

"What, then? Exactly."

"It was implied that my resignation would be accepted. I submitted it. They accepted it."

"Why?" asked Greer. "You have a distinguished reputation."

"It was a disagreement over a matter of policy. I was in the minority. A minority of one."

"And this disagreement? What did it concern?"

"There was a conflict on the direction that the research concerning the alien samples should take. They felt I was too conservative. I still feel I was right."

"Research, you say? Could you explain that to me?"

"They want to rush in without, what seems to me, adequate preparation. Scientific investigations should proceed at an orderly pace. It's dangerous to rush into things you know little about."

"Dangerous? Very interesting, Dr. Mendoza. I'd like to hear more about this. Perhaps you haven't been given a fair hearing. Would you like a seat? Here, sit down, please. I'm quite interested in scientific research."

"Raise you ten."

The others had dropped out, Brown had left a few minutes ago. Rob stared at his cards, looked up at Sam, caught his eye for a long second, went back to his cards. Full house. Queens over threes. What time was it? Sam was probably bluffing. He slid out a printed credit slip.

"Here's your ten . . . and twenty more." he pushed another slip into the middle of the table.

"It's only paper," said Sam, matching the bet. "I call."

"Full house," said Rob, spreading his cards face up carefully in front of him.

"Four tens," said Sam, casually flipping his cards onto the pile of chips, money and credit slips. "Read 'em and weep."

He raked the pile into a loose heap in front of him and dealt the next hand.

Rob was getting tired and careless. He lost four straight hands. He often misread his cards, raised when he should have called, stayed in long after he should have dropped out. What time was it? The deal rotated to him, he shuffled mechanically, cut the cards, dealt five card stud, giving himself aces back to back. He pushed money into the pot after each flip of the cards, never improving his hand. He lost to three fours and felt stupid as hell.

"Two more hands," he said. "I've got to go."

He lost them both.

Rob was opening the door to his laboratory when he remembered that he was supposed to meet Linda. He paged her in the cafeteria but she didn't answer: no wonder, he was a couple hours late. He looked for his snails. Where were they? They weren't where he thought he had left them and it took him five minutes to find the right batch.

The snails weren't ready. He puttered around a little, feeling helpless, and decided to find Linda. She was probably in her room. She'd probably be mad.

Coral reefs rise from the ocean shelf like spires of some impossible castle. A thousand colors clash and merge and clash again as layer upon layer of calcium skeletons pile themselves on top of one another from the murky depths to the mirrored surface.

Among the coral castles I/we make my/our way. Home, this is truly home. Free, weightless; movement is easy, effortless. A casual sweep of the tail, a twist of the body, a flip of a fin propels us through the water. We become I, all are one. I move, glide through the warm currents surrounded by food. Food is everywhere; plankton to be sieved, small creatures to be sucked in along with them, larger creatures to be enticed, trapped, chased. All is food, eating is constant, beauty is everywhere.

A school of something passes beneath me. They are large, brittle, spindly things, all legs, arms, antennas. Like spiders, like crabs, like shrimp made out of thin wire. I turn, dive. They seek the shelter of the coral, hiding in the shadows of its delicate branches. I catch two, eating them quickly. They are crunchy and sour, like a lemon with bones. The coral spreads out here, a ledge a hundred meters long hanging in the water like a huge fan. It looks fragile, delicate. It is stronger than iron. Under the fan I seek and find small shelled animals. Within the shells they are soft. They go down smoothly and have the taste of sulfur. It is not unpleasant.

Above, the silver surface marks the edge of the world. It moves constantly, small grasses and the warmfish cluster close to it. Rafts of seaweed occasionally drift overhead, blocking the sun, causing huge shadows to chase across this waterworld. Below is the darkness, the depths, the valleys where the sun never reaches. From the coral I drift over one of the trenches. It is bottomless. Small patches of phosphorescence flash randomly below. The darkness is inhabited only by the small and weak or the large and dangerous. It is not the home of the dragonfish. It is not my home.

Home is here. Here in the place between light and darkness. Home is the spawning flats, the cycle of tides, the storms, the food, always the food.

Home is not metal and walls. Home is the gentle tug of the currents. Home is. . . .

Metal? Walls?

Maria shook her head, looked up and down the corridor. She was alone. She was drenched in cold sweat. She had done it again.

What's happening to me?

With tears in her eyes she headed for her room, turning her back on the dragonfish, on alien worlds.

* * *

"I don't want to talk to you," said Linda. "I'm tired and I have to work tonight. I need to rest."

Rob turned on the light, sat in the chair by her bed. He was upset. Too bad.

Her life was full of upset people these days. Patients, friends, everyone had a problem. She didn't have much patience left this evening. She was tired. She just wanted to sleep. She was upset herself.

"I'm sorry," said Rob.

"Quit saying you're sorry. I don't want to hear that anymore."

"I forgot. I don't know why. I was playing cards and I lost track of time. I just forgot."

"Look, Rob." She sat up in bed. "You don't own me and I don't own you. We both have different things. Sometimes we do things together. Leave it at that for now. You don't owe me explanations of your activities and I don't owe you long conversations when I'm trying to get some sleep."

He reached out to touch her arm. She drew away.

"Linda—."

"*Goodbye, Rob.* I'll meet you at lunch tomorrow. We can talk over those goddamn sandwiches if you still feel like talking."

"But I—."

"Flip the light off on your way out." She lay back down on the bed. "Please."

She was mad. If he stayed they'd have a fight. It had happened before. He left the room, turning out the light and closing the privacy screen behind him.

"Good night," he said through the screen.

She didn't answer.

* * *

Riggs was pissed. Brown was seven minutes late relieving him on the board. When Gonzales took over later, he'd dress Brown down but good.

Still, that was only part of the problem. It wasn't just Brown, or just this time. It was happening all over the place. Little things were going wrong throughout the station, things that shouldn't be going wrong. Little things, big things. Dietary had slipped a decimal place on their last order; they'd never be able to use all that fresh lettuce, most of it would rot. Someone over in Astronomy had accidentally flashed two boxes of photographic plates. Lord knows how many people had worked on them, how much work was lost. Wayne had pushed the wrong button in the computer room and erased the wrong tape, blanked out two weeks work of twenty researchers. It was hard to coordinate the activities of so many people in the best of times, now it was getting ridiculous. Things were getting sloppy. Something would have to be done.

As he sat in his quarters, Riggs wondered what to do. He'd have to tighten things up a lot, but how? In the Service, he'd just kick a few asses and let the chain of command take care of things. This was different. Take Martin, for instance, the clown who didn't secure the crate this afternoon. He was Supply and therefore union. Practically untouchable. Their contract was air-tight and it spelled out in great detail what he couldn't do. He couldn't push him out into space, couldn't pull off his arms and legs, couldn't put him in the brig. All he could do was relieve him of duties and ship him down on the next rotation along with a strong recommendation for permanent Earthside duties. Two men out because of a silly-ass mistake by a careless person. It was really a dumb thing to have happen. On *his* station, too, by God. Things like that just didn't happen on his station.

The pencil in his hand snapped in two. He looked at it for a minute, threw it angrily into the trash.

Riggs was pissed.

Maria sat stiffly on the edge of their bed. Julia was making coffee. Two mugs sat side by side on the counter with plastic spoons sticking out of them like small white antennas. It was a comfortable room; muted colors, fluffy pillows. Classical guitar music played softly from a small recorder, the smell of coffee hung in the air. The women were close, had lived together for two years, been lovers for three. Usually they left their work outside the door. Tonight was different.

"We almost lost him." There was bitterness in Julia's voice as she poured the coffee. "Stupid. *Stupid.* A routine valve replacement. We've done a thousand of them. Stupid. You expect to lose some of the really sick ones or the old ones, but he was only 48 years old. Strong as an ox. Forty-eight! His potassium was up over *five*. He was spiking all over the place. It shouldn't have happened. Damn."

She added cream to her mug, sugar to Maria's. Years of patterns guided her hands, she didn't think about what she was doing as she stirred the coffee, leaving the spoon in Maria's mug, placing her own spoon on a small napkin. It was the way she always did it, even though Maria never used her spoon, always set it beside her mug. It was habit and stronger than reason. "Forty-eight."

Maria looked up, took the offered mug, removed

the spoon. She held the mug close to her face with both hands, sipped it twice, looked at Julia through the steam.

"Forty-eight what?" asked Maria, blinking her eyes.

"He was only 48. The man. Today's patient. The one we almost lost."

"Oh." Maria took another sip, stared at the wall, through the wall. Something was nagging at her, tugging at something deep inside her. "Have you ever been diving?" she asked. "In the ocean?"

"Scuba diving? Sure. In the keys when I was a kid. Uncle Bill lived in Key West."

"This man. Was it bad? How did it happen?"

"The patient? Everything happened so fast. He went sour. Candy caught it first. John was on the monitor and he missed the potassium. Almost lost him."

Candy. EEG. The crumpled paper.

"You hate to lose them. You've never gotten used to it," said Maria. "Have you ever been down in the reefs? Coral?"

"A few times at Pennecamp. Once in Australia. It was beautiful. I remember being cold." She sat on the edge of the counter, swinging her legs. She sipped her coffee carefully. "I don't mind the old ones. You expect to lose them once in awhile." It was a lie. She had never come to terms with death, though she faced it all the time. They both knew it was a lie.

"I remember the reefs," said Maria, staring off into space as if trying to capture an elusive memory. "They were huge, the water was warm. The things that lived there were good to eat. I never went hungry. I ate constantly."

"When you were a child? In Mexico?"

"No. Yes. I can't remember. The things I ate were very good. The water was warm, I remember that. The water was warm."

"I went really deep the time I was in Australia. The water was cold. You know, the Great Barrier Reef."

"The things I ate were good. I swam without effort."

"Australia was beautiful. I even liked the desert. I wanted to stay forever."

"Forever. That's it. *La mañana eternidad.* To swim forever. To feel the alien sun. Warm. *Caliente.*"

The music stopped. Julia slid off the counter and flipped the tape. The music that came out of the speaker was played by a man who had been dead for fifty years. The music had been written by a man who had been dead for 300 years. It was timeless, as old as yesterday, as fresh as tomorrow. They both liked it.

"Good thing Candy was there," said Julia. "Nora wouldn't have caught it so quick. He probably would have died."

"The small creatures died," said Maria. "I plucked them from the coral. They had no taste, or they were bitter, I can't remember."

"In Mexico?" asked Julia, picking up her coffee.

"Yes. No. I was young. It was yesterday, today, ten years ago. I was standing on a mountain, the sun was shining. There were two moons in the sky." Her hands shook. Coffee spilled onto her lap. She stared straight ahead, unseeing, unfeeling.

"Are you all right?" asked Julia, concerned.

"I flew with the mantas, tasted their wind—*my* wind. The snowball and I felt the first rays of the sun, dug the earth. The coral was high, the water warm."

Julia went to the side of the bed, touched Maria's face, brushed back a strand of hair.

"I think—." she began.

"No!"

"Maria."

"You. My mother. The blanket. The beach." She was gasping for breath. The mug of coffee slid from her hands. Hot coffee was everywhere.

"Madre de Dios!" Maria clawed at her chest, her legs kicked out from underneath her. Julia grabbed for her, missed. She slipped through her lover's arms to the floor.

Julia stood frozen. *My God, not her!* One second passed. *Not Maria, not now!* Two seconds. Maria was thrashing on the floor, gasping for air, not getting any. A door slid closed in Julia's mind. She was a nurse. She knew what to do. Keep calm. A patient in respiratory distress: first clear the airways. She kneeled to the patient, the lover.

"Help," she called out as she tried to hold Maria still, open her mouth. "I need help." Maria stopped struggling and stopped breathing at the same time. Her eyes were glazed, fixed straight ahead. Her body made small jerking movements.

Julia started mouth-to-mouth resuscitation. Tears dropped from her eyes and ran down Maria's unfeeling cheeks. They had to use force to pull her off in order to get Maria to the hospital sector.

The music played to an empty room. Intricate guitar sounds mingled with the muted voices outside the privacy screen. Everybody wondered what had happened. Maria's mug was in shards on the floor, the coffee still sent off faint tendrils of steam.

Linda had just come on shift when they brought

Maria in. Five hours later, Maria Rama-Diez was dead. They had done everything possible. It hadn't been enough.

Julia had to be restrained, sedated. She went into shock and was confined to a hospital bed. Something happened, she went bad and they took her into intensive care. Twelve hours later she died, gasping for breath.

Riggs sealed the station, imposed a strict quarantine. Something had gone terribly wrong.

Chapter Four

Maria's death had been a surprise. Julia's death had been a shock. From a general nervous breakdown she had undergone rapid physical degeneration. Eventually she stopped breathing. That was that. It had been messy and quick.

The autopsy took a lot longer.

The doctors were thorough and precise. Specimens were collected, tests run. Tissues were examined with great care. Complicated linkups connected the doctors on Delta III with the best specialists available on Earth. Every move of a scalpel, turn of a forcep was guided with as much thought as possible. The entire procedure was monitored, taped, analyzed. It took a long time and when it was over, the preliminary findings were discouraging, to say the least. Consensus held that the two women had died of acute respiratory failure, causative agent unknown. They had stopped breathing and had died. It was not much more than they had known from the beginning, but it had taken them two days to find that out.

During that two days they discovered that they had a much larger problem. Whatever had killed Maria and Julia was contagious. It was spreading throughout the station. Fast.

The early signs were mental rather than physical, resembling senility more than anything else. People forgot things, misremembered events from their past, made mistakes. Eventually physical involvement developed; loss of control of muscle movements, difficulty breathing.

It had hit the hospital sector hard. Several of those who had been on duty the evening that Maria and Julia were admitted were in bad shape. The worst cases were those who had been in direct contact with the two women. Three had quit breathing on their own and had been placed on respirators.

Unfortunately, the outbreak wasn't confined to the hospital sector or even to those who had been around the victims. Other infected individuals had no previous contact with any sick people. It seemed to strike randomly around the station. It had to have something to do with the mantas, but they couldn't make the connection. In the meantime, Riggs had sealed off the mantas. No one went near them. It didn't make any sense, but they had to have something to do with it. It was only a guess, but it was their best one.

Riggs was at the end of his rope. Gonzales had just been hospitalized from nervous exhaustion. The board had been cut back to phase-four operation, displaying only the most critical data. Even that was almost too much for two people and he was afraid that Brown might slip under the strain.

It was much the same all over the station. Everyone felt the strain. It was almost as if they were under siege, and in a way they were. Services were being cut back, a holding action was being fought. People were being moved like chess pieces, out of necessity, from one position to another. Riggs realized that even though he had a lot of people at his disposal, most of them had been trained in very narrow fields. They knew little or nothing beyond their specialties. The support crew; mechanics, custodial, cooks, etc., were being called on to assist in any way possible. They did what they could and Riggs was grateful. There were so many people and so few of them with any valuable training for this particular kind of situation.

Due to the shortage of hospital personnel, Riggs had pulled everyone even remotely qualified off their routine jobs in order to take care of the sick, investigate the problem, the disease. There were few fully functional people left in the hospital sector, not a whole lot left anywhere. The pulse of the station had slowed, only the most essential work was being performed. It was all they could manage under the circumstances. It seemed as though everyone was either sick or trying desperately not to get sick, avoiding contact with infected people even though they knew it didn't help. It was hard to tell when a person caught whatever it was. The person standing next to you might have it, might be capable of infecting you. The first sign was usually a mistake. Riggs was waiting for someone to make a big one. It could kill them all.

He had to make a decision soon. Both Delta I and

Delta II had offered help. Their message had been short and to the point: aid and assistance in any shape or form—hang the expense, damn the risk. They were brothers and sisters hanging in orbit, sharing a bond that only those who have broken free of Earth's gravity can share. They knew the same fears, lived the same dangers. It would be a one-way trip. They were aware that Riggs had sealed the station, that no one left. Still, they offered, and Riggs had to decide. It was not an easy decision, balancing their needs against other people's lives.

Greer, standing in Riggs' office, didn't make things any easier.

"I don't want to hear this, Riggs. I'm going down on the next shuttle. You can't do this to me. I'm not under your command." He stood in front of the captain's small desk, hands clenched, knuckles white.

The captain looked at Greer with weary eyes, the strain beginning to show. "There isn't going to be a next shuttle, Senator, until we got this thing straightened out. Two people are dead, the hospital beds are filled. I don't know what's happening here, but until we get a better handle on it, nobody leaves. Nobody."

"Damn it, you can't treat me like a hired hand. I'm an important person. I have influential friends."

"Stuff your friends. Maria Rama-Diez was an important person. Julia Carroll was an important person. We are all potential vectors of an unidentified disease. There can be no exceptions."

"I can have a chartered shuttle up here in 48 hours. They would do that for me. My friends can put pressure in the right places."

"They can pressure all they want. If they send a shuttle up, I'll send it back. Nobody leaves."

Greer glared pure hate at Riggs. He had scrambled half his life to get to a position where nobody could push him around and here was this little man telling him what he could and could not do. It didn't sit easy, but it looked like Riggs held all the cards, at least for now.

"You're a dead man, Riggs. Finished." He drew his words out slowly, forcefully. "When we get out of this, I'll see you're busted out of command . . . or worse. I'll get you for this."

"*If* we get out of this," Riggs said with a faint smile, "you're welcome to try."

Greer stormed out of the room like an angry child.

Damn fool, thought Riggs, groping in his desk drawer for some aspirin. Too many headaches, too many problems, too thin a line between them and disaster. He found the bottle, took three tablets without water, leaned back, massaged his temples, thought of his wife.

It would be night in Los Angeles, she'd be sleeping. He closed his eyes, could almost feel her steady breathing, the cat a warm lump at the foot of the bed. The house would be dark, the pump for the fish tank a faint hum in the next room. The furnace would clank loudly as it cycled off and on. He'd meant to fix the furnace a thousand times, but somehow when he was home there was never time for that.

It hadn't been much of a life for her; he was gone most of the time. They'd been married twenty years, *twenty years*, and space had been his constant mistress. Still, he loved her in a comfortable sort of way and the times they had together were very good.

She didn't know how serious the situation was. There had been other situations, other times. Most of them were over before she even found out about them, abstract events to be shared over a cup of coffee. So many times. So long ago. She lived for his rotations home. He realized there was a good chance there might not be any more.

He stood, broke his chain of thought. Almost time to relieve Brown. He walked through his side door into the board room. Brown was drenched in sweat, didn't look up. He was at the end of a double. They all pulled double shifts, it was the natural course of things these days. *Natural course?* He stared at Brown's exhausted face. *How much can he stand? How much more of this can any of us stand? Too many people, too many chances for error. Too much strain.*

He sat in his chair, activated the controls. Brown sighed audibly, coughed twice and left. The first thing Riggs did was flash Delta II to inform them that he could not justify endangering additional personnel, knowing full well that they would come anyway. He would have to turn them back, no matter how badly he needed them. It was his command, his decision. Too many decisions.

Marsha Riggs, age 42, wife, lover. Damn.

Rob looked over Jodie's shoulder as she prepared the last of the culture flasks. She worked slowly and carefully. Time was important, but accuracy was critical. They had been working around the clock for days, sleeping in bits and pieces whenever they could. Everyone did.

The schistosomes that had brought Rob to Delta III sat neglected in one corner of the lab. With Maria dead and Carlos out of the picture, Rob had found himself to be the senior bioresearcher in the station.

It was a responsibility he had definitely not sought out, one that weighed heavily on him.

He felt inadequate, unprepared. There was so much to do, so many unknown factors at play. He coordinated activities with the medical staff and kept Riggs briefed. More advice than he could possibly handle was flooding up from Earth. He had contacted Dr. Lyle, his faculty advisor, to screen things before they were sent up, but still there were too many things that couldn't be ruled out without exhaustive tests. A hundred experts would send up a hundred different avenues of attacking the problem and he only had ten or twelve people to work with. He was swamped, had to select the most promising lines of investigation or the ones most easily confirmed or ruled out. But time was slipping away. For all of them.

"They're ready," said Jodie, stepping aside so that Rob could get to the hood.

The hood was a sterile enclosure about two meters square, with a sloping glass front and an exhaust tube that vented out through the ceiling of the lab. It was an ideal place to handle infectious material under sterile conditions. It was getting a lot of use these days.

Rob sat down, inserted his hands into a complicated harness in front of the hood. He stretched his fingers experimentally and a twin pair of metal hands moved inside the hood. They looked like thin skeleton hands made of chrome, and were connected electronically to the harness. Feedback gave Rob a sense of feel nearly as acute as if he had his own hands inside the hood.

Inside the enclosure fifty small flasks were lined up

against the far wall. They contained a deep maroon layer of a blood-agar mixture about the texture of gelatin covering the bottom, with a fluid overlay of a balanced salt solution. A cotton plug capped each one. It was a fantastic culture medium, developed and refined over many years. Almost anything known could be maintained in it, at least for a short period of time. Whether or not it would culture out the organism that was loose on the station, however, remained to be seen.

Rob handled the flasks with a fluid, easy motion. He removed the stopper from the flasks, flamed the mouths over a small burner, injected each one with an amber fluid—serum from an infected individual. He talked aloud as he worked, reciting which serum sample was going into which flask. Jodie put checkmarks on a chart she was holding as he spoke. Soon he had innoculated all the flasks.

"That ought to do it," he said, rising. "Put the even numbers under oxygen and the odd ones under carbon dioxide. Smear and plate after twelve hours and every four hours after that."

Jodie nodded. "Anything else?"

"Yes. Be sure and call me after you've isolated the organism." He grinned weakly. It was a feeble joke.

"Want a miracle cure, too?"

"If you've got time." Rob walked to the sink, washed up, went to the door.

"I'll check back with you later," he said. "I'm going down to see how Hypes is doing with the chromatography. It ought to be coming off soon. If Linda calls, see when she'll be free."

Jodie watched him leave, sat down when the door closed behind him. She wiped her forehead, it was

hot in the lab. Or maybe it was her. She didn't feel
too well. She started to flush the hood, move the
flasks. There was work to be done.

It was the largest hyperbaric chamber ever built by
man and it was too small. Sam sat at the controls, as
he had for days, chewing an unlit digar. Tony was
watching over the engineering deck. Sam thought of
the *Phoenix* and how far away it seemed, how many
years ago. The cigar tasted terrible.

The *Phoenix* had been his first ship. It was special.
Like a man's first love, his first ship is something he
remembers forever. He had been raw at the time, a
drifter, a green recruit. The *Phoenix* had been a first-
class pile of junk, a converted trawler way past its
prime. It was stationed in a remote corner of the Arc-
tic Ocean to protect a small group of off-shore oil
wells from terrorist attack. It had never seen hostile
action, and, except for a couple of bar fights, neither
had Sam.

Sam and the *Phoenix* were meant for each other
from the start. Sam loved engines and the *Phoenix*
needed a great deal of attention in that department.
The engines were filthy, covered with several layers
of dirty grease. They knocked and wheezed, the
result of years of careless neglect. Sam dug in. He got
little help from the rest of the crew. Most of them
were conscripts, just doing their time, trying to get by
with as little effort as possible. If the engines gave out
and they had to be towed into port for repairs, so
much the better. Anything beat the cold endless
watches. They called the ship the *Rusty Bucket* and
laughed about it. Sam would have none of this.

Days turned into weeks and Sam came to be on in-
timate terms with the engine room. He lived most of

the time within its four small walls, never knowing or caring if it was day or night outside, if it was raining or snowing. It was always the same in his little world, warm with the gentle throbbing of the engines, steadily growing healthier under his constant care.

Deep inside the ship, Sam felt fully alive for the first time in his life. He disassembled the engines a part at a time, cleaning them, oiling them, making small adjustments. He never replaced a part until he had held it, studied it, gotten the feel of how it fit into the ship as a whole. His senses were magnified, enhanced. He felt as strong as the pistons that drove the ship. The maze of tubes and pipes slowly yielded their secrets to him. Stubbornly he traced the pipes, followed the tubes, until he knew them inside and out; better, even, than the streets of his home town. It became part and parcel of his own life; his past, his present, his future. He learned to trust his ears. A small click buried underneath the general roar of the ship while it was underway would grate his nerves until he had traced it down: a worn bushing, perhaps, a burr on a bearing that had to be filed down. He learned to trust his sense of feel; a slight vibration in the floor panels would be a counterbalance out of alignment, a rod starting to knock. He wouldn't rest until it was perfect and he had it perfect when the terrorists hit.

They hit the ship because it was between them and the oil wells they wanted to destroy. It was nothing to them but an obstacle. Sam took it as a personal affront. It was *his* ship they were attacking, *his* engines. He was everywhere, it was a blur. On the decks, in the engine room, he fought them with guns and wrenches. Everything ran together. The crew was panicked, Sam was mad. He was crazy wild, like a

dog defending his home turf. They took an armor-
piercing shell midships, in the engine room. Fire and
steam went everywhere. Somehow Sam kept it running, despite burns and blisters. In the middle of it
all, Sam was on the deck repelling boarders after the
captain fell. Everything was a red haze, Sam saw only
fury. Luckily this particular terrorist group didn't
have nukes, or if they did they were saving them for
the cluster of oil wells. It didn't matter—they took
whatever they had to the bottom. Sam blinked and it
was all over.

Out of the mess, Sam received recommendations,
awards, commendations, and a long hospital stay.
His burns healed slowly, painfully, after a series of
skin grafts. He came to the attention of the
Academy. Important people in uniforms came to talk
to him. He was given tests. They said he was officer
material.

Material? An officer? Sam wasn't too sure about
any of that. All he knew was that something very important had happened to him in the darkness of the
engine room. Something vital within him had come
to the surface. But there was more to it, there had
to be, and the only way he could get deeper into it
was by getting an education. Otherwise, he'd be a
scrubby the rest of his life. He took more tests. In the
fall he entered the Academy.

Four years later he graduated. It had been a long
four years, no doubt about it. Sam had never figured
himself to be any smarter than anyone else, but he
felt if he worked twice as hard as the rest of the class,
he might have a chance. It worked. Slowly blueprints
and schematics gave up their secrets, became engines
that lived and breathed. Pieces fell into place. A
scholarship paid his tuition, poker paid his expenses.

When he got his diploma he wasn't at the head of his class, but he didn't carry the anchor, either.

His first assignment was for submarine duty and he found it a challenge, so many new things to learn. He learned them well, too. Soon he was working with the Red Squad, an elite unit specializing in undersea rescue. It was not much later that he became second in command of the squad, working out of Newport News. It was there he first got close to a chamber.

The hyperbaric chamber had much in common with a submarine, a submarine out of water. The one in Newport News was built like a huge pressure cooker and could hold five people. The pressure inside was controlled like a submarine. It was used primarily for divers with the bends, a situation where bubbles of nitrogen had been forced into their blood system by exposure to large pressures and too rapid decompression. The patients were put into the chamber and "lowered" to pressures similar to those they had been exposed to. They were "brought up" to sea level pressure slowly, allowing the nitrogen to be replaced by oxygen.

The chamber had other uses, too. Gas gangrene, which was controlled by exposure to oxygen, could be treated in the chamber by adjusting the atmosphere to pure oxygen and running the pressure up. This method of forcing oxygen into a person's system was useful in treating several other medical conditions, including impending CVAs. Sam was trained to run the chamber during his shore rotations. They almost always used submarine personnel at the controls.

Since the chamber in Newport News was the largest one south of Baltimore, it was busy there. Sam found that he liked working with the medical staff, liked being busy, learning new things. One thing he could never do was stand still, so when the chance came to go into space, he grabbed it.

Ten years in space and here he was back at the controls of a hyperbaric chamber again. Some things never changed. The cigar tasted terrible.

Susan looked at Sam through the porthole, caught his eye.

"Ten fathoms and descending," he said. "Approaching three atmospheres at normal rate of descent. We'll hit hold point in about five minutes." His voice was flat through the small speaker inside the hyperbaric chamber.

Susan nodded. "Thanks, Sam," she said.

"Nothing to it, Ms. Walker."

Susan liked chamber work, it was one of the main reasons she'd signed up for Delta III. She had worked at the big one in Baltimore, but this was larger, better. At least when things were normal, when they didn't have the fine edge of panic, like now.

Normally, the chamber in Delta III was used as a routine tool in the recovery procedure for the open heart surgery that was performed at the station. Occasionally operations came up that were better performed under the high pressure oxygen environment available in the chamber. They got the worst of the gas gangrene patients. It was not unusual for a couple of them a month to be shipped up from Earth. The research people also used the chamber a lot.

Five decompression cases had been treated in the chamber since Susan had first come up. They'd been bad. Accidents in space tended to be quick and unforgiving.

Now the chamber was in use twenty-four hours a day and a feeling of urgency ran high in the team. They couldn't treat the disease, whatever it was that was loose on the station, but they could work on the symptoms, particularly when it reached the stage where the patients stopped breathing on their own. It was a two-pronged attack. First they would get the patient on a respirator, let a machine do his breathing for him. Next they would get him into the chamber as soon as possible. The high pressure not only forced oxygen into the patient's system, but his blood could hold more of it than was normally possible. The effect lasted as long as the patient was in the chamber and for a short time afterwards. Ideally, the patient should be kept constantly in the chamber, but that wasn't possible. Besides possible oxygen toxicity complications, there were simply too many patients. The chamber only held ten people at a time, twenty if you stacked them, and it was always full. People rotated in and out. They steadily got worse, eventually died. There was nothing else they could do at this stage.

Susan was used to crisis situations, it was one of the things that had drawn her to nursing. At Trauma she had seen a lot, grown up quick. She had been at the Cape that time the shuttle blew up on the pad. After all that, she felt that nothing could get to her. She was wrong.

This new situation was getting to her, though she wouldn't admit it. Nobody ever got any better, nobody got well and walked away. There was only the steady stream of patients slowly getting worse and worse, never improving, never showing any signs of recovery, just a gradual decline to death. They were all people she knew, worked with. Life was a closed circle on Delta III. It was impossible not to wonder if you would be next. Most of the nurses were down, it had hit them hard. Treating an infectious disease that had an unknown causative agent and an unknown method of transmission was a risky business. They shared the risk and plowed ahead. One by one they all dropped, doctors and nurses right alongside their patients. At times it seemed hopeless, that they'd all die up here. When she felt that way Susan did the only thing she could do—she gritted her teeth and worked harder. Work pushed the dying a little farther away.

The chamber kept her busy, drove away the fears. Still, it didn't cure anyone, just kept them alive a little while longer. It was at best a holding action, but it was the only action they had.

They were both preoccupied. Rob's head was full of figures, loose ends of experiments in progress. Linda was trying to switch gears. She had spent the morning being a psychologist and would spend the afternoon being a nurse. It was always a bit of a jolt. Sometimes she felt like she wore too many hats.

They sat quietly at the edge of the deserted zero-g exercise area, sharing the silence, sharing the feeling of being close. A handball paddle hung in the middle of the court, rotating slowly, end over end. Nobody worked out here anymore; no time, no energy. Rob had his arm around Linda, she had her head on his shoulder. They watched the paddle spin and didn't feel the need to speak. They were that close.

A loose strand of Linda's hair brushed Rob's face and triggered memories, old memories. Porpoises at play. Sunrise over the ocean. Hand in hand in the salt spray. The wind off the ocean was cold in the morning, they were wearing shorts and t-shirts, shivering a little, holding hands, holding each other. A line of pelicans dipped and rose along the water's edge. Gulls huddled on the sand facing the wind, wings drawn in tight. Each shell was special. Like children they would pick them up, wash them in the surf, show them to each other, hold them, marvel at the colors, the many shapes, the way the ocean had worn them down. Then they would put them away and months later, a continent apart, she or he would open a box and there would be a shell, just an ordinary seashell, but so much more.

A fine summer. They had just finished pre-med together. There were six short weeks before they went their separate ways for awhile. God, how young they'd been. Six weeks. So many things said, so many things done. Moments stood out.

Sipping beer in a bar on a dune above the ocean. A woman jogging along the empty beach below them, two dogs at her side. Doberman pinchers. The bar had once been a Coast Guard rescue station, thick overhead beams, sun-weathered wood on the outside. It was their favorite bar, miles from anywhere. Ships sailed by on the edge of the ocean. They gave them strange names and exotic destinations, made up stories about their captain and crew. They laughed easily, like children.

A day sailing on a rented catamaran, quietly cutting through the water of a large protected bay. A mangrove island among other mangrove islands; isolated, a small sandy beach. Skinny-dipping, running naked across the island, lazy love, crazy things. Started back too late, the wind was wrong. Tacking took a long time. Darkness came and with it the small churning in the pit of the stomach; fear as old as man, fear of the dark, fear of the unknown. Slowly, the lights of the marina came into view. There had been no real danger, but the owner was relieved to see them just the same. A couple of beers in the motel bar, a few more stories to share between them. More things to bond them together.

The last day of the summer. He off to Hopkins, she to UCLA. Different paths, an uncertain future. They walked up the beach for the last time, turned shells with their toes. They pretended time was standing still, but both of them felt each tick of the clock; each crash of surf was another moment gone forever. They sat on a dune and watched the waves come and go. Time drifted. Life could be so simple at times, so complex at others. They talked of sailing around the world, of chucking it all and finding an island to live on. They were playing, but while they were playing, doors were sliding shut in their heads. They were locking things away, getting ready to face the future.

As Rob had unpacked his suitcase in his new apartment in Baltimore, a starfish fell from one of his folded shirts. He picked it up, sat on the bed and thought of Linda so many miles away. He wondered when she'd find the shell necklace he'd hidden in her bag.

He smiled at the memory, shifted his position slightly. The paddle still hung in the air.

Linda watched it rotate, spin. Time stretched out. It was good to sit with Rob and think of things besides death, or think of nothing at all. She could relax with Rob, no facades, no masks, no games. The years had given them that much, at least; more, in fact. With Rob she could be herself, good and bad. He understood. Most of the time, anyway.

Sometimes . . . well, they were both human, with all their human faults and failings. She knew she tended to get impatient and irritable if things didn't go right. Sometimes she was bitchy. Rob could get so involved in his work that he would forget everything else. Sometimes he seemed distant. They both loved their work, it was a part of their lives. There were other things, too. Things they shared. Things they had done together.

They had met at the University of Kansas. She had been his lab partner in Zoo 104, a comparative anatomy course. She had been—how old—eighteen, nineteen? So long ago. Somewhere between the shark and the frog he had asked her out. They were sophomores. They had three good years together. Long nights of studying, lots of coffee and too little sleep. A few parties, lots of long walks, football games. All the usual stuff made a little special by being with someone special. She remembered the dog. Skippy. The color of peanut butter. They found him by the side of the road that night. Someone had hit him and left him for dead. Rob held him in his lap as she drove to the veterinarian. Two broken legs and head injuries. Light peanut butter with a little white around the throat. A mixed breed, a mongrel. His legs healed, but the head injuries left him subject to fits. They loved him, cared for him. He died the week before graduation with his head in Linda's lap. He died quietly. He had been a fine dog.

Linda pressed closer to Rob. With him she didn't have to be strong all the time. It was hard to be strong in the face of so much death. She thought of Skippy. She felt like a little girl. It was good to feel little once in a while.

It all seemed so hopeless.

She looked up at Rob and there were tears in her eyes.

He kissed them away.

Riggs tossed in his sleep. Mantas chased him across an endless desert. The sun was hot, he couldn't get good footing. They (it was a pair, it was always a pair) swooped down on him, knocking him end over end. Sand in his mouth, in his eyes. His feet were raw, covered with blisters, his body covered with scratches. The sun was hot. He would get to his feet only to be knocked down again. Always the same, over and over. He kicked the covers from his bed, the dream slipped away. It would return. It always did.

Jodie started the run. It was the fifth run she had done today on the amino acid analyzer. She inserted the sample into the top of the column and started the timers. Pumps wheezed and the pressure built, slowly forcing the sample through the tightly packed column.

It took two hours to make a complete run, using both the long column and the short one. That was the big problem with this particular machine; it took so long. The best they could do was twelve samples a day. Out of how many?

She looked at the flasks in the cold box. Must be fifty in there. More came in every day. It was an assortment of different patients or the same patient on different days. They'd never catch up at this rate. She shrugged to herself. The other selected what samples to run, all she did was babysit the machine.

It was a nice machine, but slow. If a person were

sick, they usually showed an amino acid imbalance. By checking which amino acids were out of line, it was conceivably possible to trace backwards to find out *why* they were wrong. It might provide a handle on the disease. Maybe. Jodie had her doubts. Amino acids had complicated cycles, many factors could cause an imbalance. The results were often ambiguous and it wasn't possible to run enough samples to get a large, overall picture. The analyzer was primarily used for research. Research in which they had plenty of time. That simply wasn't the case right now. Still, it was her job and she didn't complain.

As the recorder needles started to move, Jodie wrote on the chart: sample number, patient's name, today's date, date of sample, method of preparation of sample, run number, time. She initialed the run in the corner of the paper. Nothing to do now but wait. The needles traced lines in blue, red and green ink.

There was a knock on the door and Jodie swung around to see Rich entering with a wire rack of tubes. More samples.

"This morning's goodies," he said.

"Morning?" she said. "Could have sworn it was the middle of the night."

"It's morning to me," said Rich. "Got in my eight hours of sack and I'm ready to go."

"Ugh," said Jodie. Rich was always cheerful. It was disgusting. "Set them over there." She waved a weary arm in the direction of the bench. "I'll get to them in a minute."

"Whatever you say, my dear." He set them down with an exaggerated sweep of his arm. "Anything to please." He bounced to the door.

"And speaking of pleasing," he said, half out the

door. "What are you doing after you get off work?"

"*If* I ever get off work, I'm headed straight to bed."

Rich raised one eyebrow.

"Alone," she said firmly.

"Can't blame a guy for trying," he said with a smile.

"Oh yes I can. Goodbye."

"I'll be seeing you."

"No doubt," she said as he closed the door.

Jodie shook her head. More work. Seemed like nothing ever ended, everything just kept going in one long blur. The charts and tables she kept were her only way of making some order out of the chaos. The tidy lists of names, samples and tests were an anchor for her, something concrete to hold on to while everything else swirled around her. She stood up and walked over to the samples Rich had brought.

Blood samples. Today's patients. She copied down more names and numbers from the stoppered tubes, slipped them in the centrifuge, set the timer for ten minutes. A low whine, muted, joined the noise of the amino analyzer's pumps. Jodie sat down and reached for her cup of tea. Cold. Damn. Nothing went right. For a moment she wished she shared a little of Rich's optimism, Rob's determination and stamina.

While she waited for the timer on the centrifuge, she half dozed in her chair, drifted a little bit. With the background noise and her eyes closed, she could almost imagine herself back in the lab at Community, years away, a lifetime ago. Much simpler times. She rested and wondered if Thelma was still there, plugging away. Whatever happened to Larry?

A small noise intruded, a creak. She opened her eyes. It was masked by the noise of the centrifuge, she couldn't quite make it out. She looked around the room. Nothing . . . nothing . . . *there.* The pressure gauge on the amino acid analyzer was pegged. She'd forgotten to set the safety. She jumped to the machine to hit the emergency vent. Too late.

The two glass columns on the front of the machine exploded under the pressure, shards of glass flew everywhere. Something short-circuited with a crackle, smoke filled the lab.

Jodie was covered with hundreds of tiny cuts, but she didn't realize it. She had made a mistake. It was her fault. She was covered with blood, it didn't matter. She was crying, but the pain hadn't hit yet.

My fault. Both columns gone. All that work. So much smoke. Replacements from Earth. Take forever. All that work. My God, the blood. The pain! No. No. God! The blood.

It took three minutes for Jeff to come from the lab next door and drag her out. It seemed like hours. He didn't know where to touch her, there was so much blood. She was still crying. There was a lot of smoke.

. . . and as we said in yesterday's broadcast, it is not that the space stations themselves are inherently dangerous, it is only that they are mismanaged and without proper safeguards. Their own senior scientists seem to agree. (*cut from full face to stock footage of space station laboratory*) Doctor Carlos Mendoza was quoted the other day as saying that the research being carried out there was irresponsible. Events seem to have proven him correct. (*fade to long shot of station*) Just what do we have up there above our heads? (*pan back, music up*) Is it something that will save mankind? (*freeze frame*) Or will it kill us all? (*quick cut to announcer, full face, music OUT*) Legislation was introduced this morning on Capitol Hill to take emergency measures concerning the space station. The UN is currently in a special session debating the recent developments and their possible consequences. Meanwhile, Arnold Greer, senior senator from New Jersey and presidential hopeful, is being held a virtual prisoner on . . .

Rob crumpled the paper and tossed it into the recycler. Another dead end. Jeff's group had come up empty handed. They'd have to step back again, take another tack. More time lost.

Where should he have them turn? His desk was littered with suggestions from scientists on Earth. He didn't even feel qualified to judge them, much less supervise the carrying out of the plans. Jeff was just a technician and the people working under him had little or no training. They were crew members who had been drafted for the job and had to be watched closely. How did they expect to get anywhere?

Walking over to his sink, Rob splashed cold water on his face, tried to collect himself. *Wrong. Have to be positive. We have fine equipment here, the best. Good people. The best minds on Earth are working with us. We have a chance. Slim. A chance. We can do it. We have to do it.*

Rob started to call the computer people, changed his mind, decided to walk over and see them. The walk might clear his head.

The halls were deserted. On the way over he only passed four people and they looked distracted, preoccupied. His footsteps echoed hollowly. He felt very much alone, like walking though a department store after closing or, better perhaps, along the deck of the *Mary Celeste.*

As many times as Rob had been there, he always felt like an interloper in the computer room. They were strange people; it was almost as if they spoke a different language, lived in a different world. The only one of them that he knew very well was Ray, they'd played cards a few times before all this happened. In contrast with the deserted hallways, the computer room was full of activity. He stood in the doorway looking lost for a second, saw Ray's bushy head across the room and headed for him.

"Ray," he said. "Got anything for me?"

"We're hooked into Beltsville now," he said. "Want to watch?"

Rob nodded and Ray led him over to a terminal. Numbers were flashing by on the screen faster than he could follow them. A printout was clacking out underneath the screen, paper piling on top of paper. The sheets were packed with numbers too. None of it made any sense to Rob.

"What is all this stuff?" asked Rob.

Ray laughed. "It's your enzymes from this morning. They're running an analysis of variance."

Rob stared at the top sheet, squinted his eyes as if by looking harder he could make some sense out of it, make the truth jump out. He failed miserably. They were still just a bunch of numbers. They didn't mean anything.

"I don't understand this, Ray."

"It's simple," he said, tearing off a sheet. "These are patient numbers, these are the enzymes you test for, coded of course, and these are the test results." He moved his finger to another column. "These are normal ranges, these are mean values, these are standard deviations, these are the first order interactions. Pretty soon we'll have the final level of significance. This is really the machine talking to itself, or Beltsville's machine talking to our machine, really.''

"Really?" asked Rob. He couldn't keep the sarcasm out of his voice. Ray missed it completely.

"Yeah," said Ray. "Here it comes now." The machine stopped typing.

"What does it show?" asked Rob.

"Nothing. Nothing out of line. All values within accepted limits.''

Rob shrugged his shoulders. He hadn't really expected anything.

"Of course, now we have to tag these against yesterday's results,'' said Ray. "And then we'll run a compilation of all the enzymes run to date. Should have it on your desk within an hour.''

"Thanks, Ray," said Rob.

"Anything you want. Just let us know.''

Rob patted Ray on the back, thanked him again, and walked out the door. He paced the halls for awhile, thinking. There was something wrong here, but he couldn't put his finger on it. The computers were fast, they were accurate, but they were dumb. They were simple-minded, narrow-minded machines. For the thousandth time he reminded himself that computers didn't think for themselves, they only carried out instructions. They could only do what they had been told to do. If the instructions weren't precise, the results weren't reliable.

The computer could tell if something was statistically significant, but what did that really mean? There was a point where the figures interfaced with the living systems. Unless you rode herd on the computer it was possible something biologically significant might slip by. If an event happened only once, the computer might round it off, average it out, or even throw it away. But it might be important, biologically important, vitally important. Something might pop out in the flood of numbers and not be recognized by the computers. Many of the lab people working now had so little knowledge of the things they were measuring that almost anything could slip by them. The test results didn't mean anything more to them than they did to the computer. Both of them saw the results only as numbers, not in terms of the living systems.

He headed back to the computer room. He'd have to get Ray to explain the program even if it took all night or longer. They might have to run everything through again. It would take some time, but it would be worth it. He was excited as he hadn't been for days.

Linda sat with Susan in the nurses' lounge. Rob was late. Again. She'd been waiting twenty minutes for him, fifteen minutes more than she figured she should have. Susan was coming off a double. She was tired.

"Why don't you go sack out, get some rest?" asked Linda.

"Got to do reports," said Susan. "Just wanted to get off my feet for a few minutes first. My back is killing me. Since they moved those last two stretchers into the chamber, there isn't any place to sit down. Had some bad ones today. Went down to ten atmospheres, took us five hours to decompress. On my feet the whole time."

Linda nodded. There wasn't anything to say. They

all did that these days. She was headed into the chamber in a few minutes herself. Damn Rob, he wasn't in his room or in the labs, she'd called. If he said he'd meet her, he damn well ought to show up or at least try to get in touch with her. "I've got the next chamber shift," she said. "Spellings is going in with me."

"That's right," said Susan dully. "I remember. Warren is in charge. You know him? Dr. Martinez?"

"Vaguely. I've never worked with him."

"You'll have to watch him. He's slow. They dragged him in from someplace in Research. He's not really prepared for this, hasn't practiced in years. Hates to make decisions. Afraid to, maybe."

"I can understand that," said Linda. "It's been awhile since my nursing days. Sometimes I don't feel qualified at all."

Susan reached over and laid a hand on Linda's leg. "You're doing fine, a great help. Wish we had more like you."

Linda dropped her hand to Susan's and squeezed it. "I don't see how you hold up."

"Just like everyone else, one foot after the other. We just keep going."

The door to the lounge opened. "The doctors are ready for reports, Ms. Walker."

Susan stood. "Coming along?"

"Sure," said Linda. "Anything special?"

"Keep a close eye on Lindquist, she's going bad. Arrested twice last shift. Be careful suctioning her."

"Okay." Sara Lindquist was a statistician. They'd worked together a lot. Damn it all.

"How's Rob?" asked Susan as they left the room.

"Don't ask," replied Linda, not bothering to hide the bitterness in her voice. Damn him. Damn it all.

*   *   *

It was easier with two people.

One person could, in a pinch, get into a suit alone, but it went a lot faster if somebody helped you. It took a lot of cooperation and patience, neither of which was much in evidence among the men on the loading platform. They milled about, got in each other's way. Most of them were way past their normal rotation time and not very happy about it. They grumbled a lot, but there wasn't much they could do about it. They were stranded on Delta III just like the scientists.

"Hurry up. The shuttle's waiting."

"It can blinking well wait. I'm not ready. Help me with this snap."

"Hey over there, hook your tether."

"I'm hooking it. Give me a chance, will you?"

"Move it, move it. Come, hurry up ."

"Don't push me. You're not my boss."

"I am right now, and if you don't get hopping, I'll kick your ass out the door."

"You can shove it, fella. Get off my back."

"Cut the chatter, boys," said a voice over the loudspeaker. "Give me a suit check. Frank—your temp's a little on the low side, nothing to worry about. Jim—cut back on your oxygen a little, it's running rich. That's better. Keep it cool, boys. We've all got a job to do."

The crew was shorthanded, tempers were rough, nerves on the raw side. It was a duty no one wanted. Since the shuttle didn't dock anymore, everything had to be transferred by grapple and manhandled into place. It was tedious, strenuous, dangerous work.

"Venting. The count is ninety."

Gradually the bay doors slid open, revealing the

shuttlecraft drifting alongside. Its top was flipped
and the spider-like crane was in place, holding the
first crate. Not too much coming aboard this time.
Ought to go quickly. But not necessarily smoothly.

"Watch it, buddy. That's fragile equipment."

"Can it. I know my job."

"Then do it. Quit griping."

Not smoothly at all.

Riggs flipped off the monitor and sighed deeply.
Morale was slipping, something had to be done.
Some people were holding up well, others were
having trouble. He couldn't blame anyone. It was
hard fighting a holding action against an enemy they
couldn't see, couldn't even identify. At times it
seemed as if they were all just waiting to die.

The situation on Earth didn't help matters at all.
Things were really boiling down there. It had its effect on Delta III in both obvious and subtle ways.
Obvious because of all the static he was getting, the
questions he had to field, the way Ground Control
had to have a conference on everything he asked.
Subtle because the last shuttle shipment was short.
The one before had been short, too. Requisitions
were being delayed, questioned. It had never happened before. He felt like he was fighting battles on
two fronts at the same time.

One was enough.

"Your computer rejected *this*?" Rob spread the
printout on the desk, circled an obscure number
buried in a mass of more obscure numbers.

"Sure," said Ray. "Look at it. It's way out of line
with the others. Obviously an error."

"I don't think so," said Rob, trying to keep his

voice calm, trying to keep anger and hope from choking him completely. "This sample ws taken less than five hours before the patient's death. We could be seeing something very specific here. Let me see the patient's electrolytes for the 48 hours before he died."

"They were taken hourly, weren't they?" asked Ray, punching numbers into the computer.

"They should have been." *And this should have been caught, too,* thought Rob. It all comes of using untrained people. They don't know when a value is significant. They just plug in the samples and read off the results. They don't know what the results mean. But there's no other way to do it. Not enough qualified people.

"Here they are," said Ray, ripping off a short sheet of paper, handing it to Rob.

"*Damn*! Look at this potassium shift. He's all out of balance. No wonder. . . . Hey, I've got to check this out."

Rob grabbed up the papers and rushed towards the door where he collided with Candy, the EEG technician.

"Rob," she said, "I've been looking all over for you." She waved a tracing in his face. "I've got—"

"Electrolytes," he shouted.

"Metabolic encephalopathy," she said excitedly.

"Neurochemical breakdown. Let's go." He grabbed Candy's arm and dragged her down the hall after him.

Ray shook his head. Those biologists were all crazy. He'd take a computer any day.

Desert. Sweeping sand piled dune upon dune. The endless search for food. Life. Death.

Companionship. Mating. Birth. The role of provider. The freedom of skies without boundaries, wings spread wide. The breezes, the high winds, the storms, the rain in the mountains. The comfort of a mate at wingtip, soaring together, diving together, a lifetime together of living together. The sounds that mean hunger. The sounds that mean contentment. The sounds that mean unrest. The sounds that mean anger. The touch of familiarity that comes after many seasons, many rains. All the feels, the sounds.

There is no sound for fear.

The male manta shifted on his perch, moved closer to his mate. Her time was approaching, soon there would be three. The strange creatures no longer came among them, though he could feel their presence. He did not allow himself the full sleep. The urge to protect was strong in him. When he dozed, the slightest sound would wake him.

When he dozed, he dreamt of endless deserts, blowing sand.

Chapter Five

Greer turned away from the port, unimpressed by the spinning Earth below. Such a ridiculous situation to be stuck in, trapped in a tin can like this. They ought to send everyone down to Earth where they had decent doctors, or at least ship a few competent doctors up here. Nobody on the station had any sense at all, especially that clown Riggs, sitting tucked away on his little throne tossing his weight around. A little tin god. Well, this was one man who didn't particularly want to be one of his subjects.

"Excuse me, Senator. Your call is coming in." That was Mike Hickson, his secretary, aide, and confidant. Never went anywhere without him.

"I'll take it in my room."

"Do you want it scrambled?"

Greer just glared at him. He should know by now.

"I'll set it up," Mike said quickly, turning back towards the room.

Greer looked out the port at the swirling clouds

that covered the Earth. That was where man belonged, not up here. He waited a moment to give Mike time to set things up, then he too headed down the hall.

The Senate Minority Leader's head filled the small vidscreen on the desk. He didn't look happy.

"It's a difficult position, Arnold, but not an impossible one." He glanced to his left at something off screen. "Public opinion is pretty well mixed."

"I'm not interested in public opinion polls, I just want to get out of here."

"You'd *better* pay attention to them. You can bet a lot of other people are. It could go either way. Some folks, lots of them, think you guys are all heros. They're really pulling for you. As long as you stay up there."

"Don't mess with me, Mark. What's that supposed to mean?"

"It means they like their heros at a distance. Martyrs, even. They're afraid. They don't want whatever you guys got to get loose down here. They love you. As long as you stay where you are."

"Great."

"On the other hand, there are people who think you're being sold down the tube, that you ought to be pulled from the station and treated in the quarantine center in Galveston."

"I've been pulling for that too, but that bonehead Riggs just won't listen to reason. I've tried all the pressure I can from up here. If we're going to do it, it'll have to be done from your end."

"We've been trying. Got a lot of mileage out of that doctor of yours. We've been seeding the news media pretty thoroughly. There's a convenient strike at the Cape. I won't say who engineered it, but it's helping bog things down. If you have any other suggestions, I'd be glad to hear them." He leaned back with a thin, superior smile. Smug son'bitch. Ought to be him that's stuck up here.

"Lean on them, pull out all the stops. Block Riggs and whatever he comes up with. Make it impossible for him to do anything but get us out of here."

"We've tried that. Riggs is clean as a whistle, war hero, stuff like that. Besides, he's like a captain of a ship at sea. He's got absolute command. It would take the President to override him."

Greer was thoughtful for a second, hunched over the vidscreen. "Then we'll have to get the President."

Mark Owens laughed. "You've gone crazy. That's it; you've caught the bug."

"Lay off, Mark. Call Mary. Have her pull my confidential file on Blassiter. Use it. That old bastard's got the President's ear. He'll crumble."

"Blassiter, huh? Chief of staff. You really got something big on him? I've been trying for years and he always came up smelling like roses."

"It's big and he buried it well. Use it."

"Okay," Mark nodded, stroked his chin. "That might do the trick. It's worth a shot."

"While you're at it, keep leaning on the papers and newscasts. You know, play the disease down, emphasize the fact that we're trapped here. Play on their sympathy. The whole bit."

"We can handle it. Blassiter. Damn. I never would have guessed."

"How do I look down there?"

"You're golden, no matter what happens. All this publicity has blown your recognition factor sky high. The nomination's in your pocket."

"First I have to get down alive."

"There is that problem," said Mark. "And another. A third group of people would like to have their way."

"Who?"

"Some old friends of yours—the anti-space contingent. You've been playing them like violins for years and now they've turned on you. Ironic, isn't it?"

"What's ironic?"

"They'd just as soon have you all die up there."

"Thanks a lot for the cheering news. Get busy."

He broke the connection with an angry stab of his hand.

Rob sat at one end of the conference table, nervous and excited. Dr. Mellon, as head of the medical staff, sat at the other end. Ed Brown, representing the captain, sat next to Rob. The others sat wherever they could, or leaned against the wall. It was crowded, hot. This was the first time so many people had showed up for one of the daily briefings. This was also the first time that anyone had anything positive to say and they didn't want to miss it.

"It's not much, but it's something," Rob was saying. "At least we know what it is that we're fighting."

Everyone was talking at once. There was something electric in the air.

Dr. Mellon called for quiet by tapping his pipe against his coffee cup. It was an unusual display of emotion for him. But these were unusual times.

"You were saying, Rob?"

"Thank you, Lee. I'll try not to get too technical."

Rob opened a folder in front of him, moved some papers around.

"As we suspected, the organism originated from the mantas. The mist secreted by the male manta, to be precise. It is anaerobic and gram positive, much like a spore or bacterium. In the female manta it inhibits bleeding, facilitates birth and the continuation of the species. In man, however, it faces its own alien environment."

"Excuse me, Rob," said Ed Brown. "This may be stupid, but do you mean to say that all this is due to that spray or whatever from the mantas?"

"That's right, Ed. The point of initial infection must have come when Maria was exposed to the manta's atmosphere. It's spread from there. You see, without this organism the female manta would bleed to death giving birth, since the young manta claws its way out through her body. The problem comes up when the organism gets into a human body. Things aren't right for it there, so it starts looking for a place that *is* right. It wanders blindly through an infected person's body, searching without success for a certain combination of biological factors, factors only to be found in the female manta. It eventually encapsulates itself in the patient's tissue. This is where the real trouble begins." Rob paused, messed with his papers. The room had grown quiet.

"After it encapsulates, it begins to secrete neurotoxins. This is purely a defensive action on the part of the organism. Yet these neurotoxins, along with the body's reaction to them, cause all the damage. The neurotoxins selectively block neural transmission at the synapses. Normal memory pathways and thought processes are disrupted. This ac-

counts for the clinical manifestations of acute confusion in the patients. Alternate pathways open up,
creating false memories, hallucinations, the apparent
senility.''

Linda and Candy, sitting together, nodded to each
other. They'd both started picking these signs up,
now that they knew what they were looking for.

''By this time the body's defense mechanisms are
in full swing. This is the other part of the problem.
Because of the totally alien nature of the organism,
the body has no frame of reference in reacting to it.
Therefore, it pulls out all the stops. Plays all the
cards in its deck, so to speak. It throws everything it
has against the organism. Many of these reactions are
self-defeating. They weaken the body, make it more
susceptible to the neurotoxin's activity. Vital functions become impaired, especially respiratory ones,
and the patient dies.''

Dr. Mellon took it all in, nodded. The human body
was a complicated system. Sometimes the things it
did weren't in its best interest. ''Rob,'' he said. ''Do
you have any idea how we can stop the body from
reacting so violently?''

Rob shook his head. ''We're nowhere near that
yet. It might be possible to suppress some of the
defense mechanisms, but that might create more
problems than it solved.''

''You said the organism is anaerobic. Doesn't that
mean it can't survive in an oxygen environment?''
asked Linda. ''How is it transmitted?''

''It's pretty adaptable and not perfectly anaerobic,
as we understand it. You've got to keep in mind that
this is an alien form, it doesn't have to conform to
the same biological patterns we do. Exposure to
oxygen doesn't kill it, except maybe under extreme

conditions like in the chamber. Concentrated amounts of oxygen seem to kill most of the exposed organisms, but not the internal ones. In a normal atmosphere it becomes dormant, like a spore. It can easily be transmitted by bodily contact or simply through the air. Once inside an infected person, it becomes active again."

"But you can't culture it yet, can you?" asked Dr. Mendoza.

"Not really, Carlos," said Rob. "We can keep it going in culture, but we haven't been able to get it to grow or reproduce. We don't even know for sure that it does grow or reproduce. Due to its rapid spread through the station, it would seem likely, but we just don't know for sure. All we've been able to do so far is identify it and maintain it. We're trying it in experimental animals now."

"You don't know what will happen to them, do you?" asked Carlos.

"Well, we're looking for various things. We hope—."

"You don't *know*, do you?"

"No. We wouldn't have to—."

"I think there's a great deal about this organism you don't know."

"I'm afraid you're right, Carlos. I'm afraid you're absolutely right."

Everybody started talking at once.

Jodie had been working all day trying to collect organisms to culture. It was tedious work, she'd been doing it for hours. She was almost finished.

The usual methods of collection—floatation, sedimentation, centrifugation—didn't work with these organisms. It tended to disrupt their cellular

makeup, tear them apart. It was strange how it could
be so resilient to some things and yet so fragile to
others. They had been forced to collect them by
direct examination of the patient's tissue; obtained
by biopsy or, more commonly, autopsy. The tissue
had to be gently pressed between two glass slides and
examined under a low-power dissecting microscope.
She scanned the tissue for localized areas of inflammation, which she removed when she found
them. The areas of inflammation were closely
examined on a wet stage under a high-power
microscope. Usually they were negative. Only about
one time in twenty or thirty did she find one of the
alien organisms in the tissue.

When she did find one, she removed it with the
micromanipulators, almost microscopic dissecting
tools made of platinum or finely drawn threads of
glass. The tools were controlled by a complicated
system of gears that reduced Jodie's hand motions by
a factor of several thousand. Slowly she would tease
the tissue apart, searching for the organism. When
she found it, she'd insert a special syringe with an extremely fine glass needle. Separating the organism
from the surrounding tissue, she'd draw it into the
needle of the syringe; transfer it carefully through a
series of sterile washes and finally place it into a
culture flask. The entire procedure was carried out
under the strictest possible isolation conditions.
Everything had to be absolutely sterile to protect the
organism and to protect the personnel from the
organism.

Rob, dressed in white isolation gear, a mask over
his face, entered the room. "How many today?" he
asked.

"This is number twenty-five."

"Good work, Jodie. That ought to do it. Have you found any sites with multiple infections?"

"No. I've had lots of patients with more than one organism, but they're always spread out. Never more than one at any location."

"Too bad. It would tell us a lot."

"How did the oxygen tolerance experiment go last night?"

"Just about as we expected. An exposed organism can survive up to 80% oxygen. At 100% they all die. That explains why more people aren't infected in the chamber. That's probably the safest place to be, all things considered."

Jodie flicked off the microscope light. "Maybe we all ought to move into the chamber," she said.

Rob stared at her. Chamber. She just might have something there.

"I want you to hyperventilate for me now," said Candy. "Take very deep breaths and blow out hard each time you exhale. Pant like a dog, that's it, you've got it. You might find yourself getting dizzy. Maybe your hands will tingle a little. Don't worry about it. That's a perfectly normal reaction."

The lights in the room were dim. The patient was lying on a small bed, a mass of multicolored wires running from his head to a complicated machine covered with tiny switches and small red and green lights. Candy stood in front of the machine, making notes on the recorder paper as it moved under the colored pens. She was running an EEG on the patient, an electroencephalograph. The tracings on the paper gave a picture of the electric activity of his brain. As he hyperventilated, she picked up a slowing in his temporal regions. Normal. Theta waves started to pick up, then delta. Not unusual. The delta waves grew in intensity, their tops were being chopped off. She cut down the sensitivity and watched them for a minute. The only sounds in the room were the patient's heavy panting and the quiet swish of the paper. Normal.

"That's enough, Paul," she said. "Breathe like you normally do." She waited a minute while his tracings recovered. She reset the sensitivity, stepped around to the patient.

"I'm going to flash a light in your eyes," she said. "You'll probably like it." She swung a chrome-faced strobe down in front of him, adjusted it so that it was about ten inches in front of his eyes. "Most people see colors or patterns when I do this. Others see shapes. Some people say it's like being high, but of course I wouldn't know about *that*." She smiled at the patient and he grinned weakly back. They were always a little nervous about all this. She went back in front of the machine.

"I want you to close your eyes now," she said. "That diffuses the light over the surface of the retina, gives us a better picture."

After he had settled down she gave him three single flashes. Looked good. Then she gave him a burst at five cycles per second, waited, hit him again with a burst of ten cps, close to his alpha frequency. Then she ran it up to fifteen and twenty. She observed the photic driving effect, his EEG frequency followed the flash frequency. Not much else, though.

His name was Paul Davis, age 32. He was a technician working with the exobiologists. Linda had referred him to her. He claimed he could read the mantas' minds.

Strange.

The board was relatively quiet. Any functions that could be shunted to other stations or Ground Control had long ago been transferred. Even with so much shifted to auto mode, the load was tremendous under the circumstances. Riggs, isolated in the board room, contacted reality only through his dials, his screens. The only person he ever came close to was Ed Brown and that was only for a few seconds when he relieved him at the board. Riggs considered even that too much of a risk. Soon he'd have to take it all over by himself.

Isolation. He felt it bitterly. He was doubly isolated from the others; first by the isolation of command and secondly by the physical barriers he had erected to keep him functional, an uninfected part of the machine. He had to keep going, it was their only hope. Riggs felt like he was the last link to the heartbeat of the station. If anything went wrong with him, it was all lost. He waited for his first mistake, the sign that they were all finished. He sometimes wondered if he'd already made it and was simply unaware of it.

The others were isolated, too. The whole station formed a series of concentric circles around the most seriously infected. Various degrees of isolation existed throughout the station. The sick moved among the sick, like some modernized form of leper colony. Through air locks and decontamination centers they walked among those with a degree of infection that matched their own. It was a one-way trip as they moved slowly toward the center; to the wards, the chamber, death.

The weekly shuttle from Earth was a life-support system for Delta III, bringing equipment, food, supplies; anything they needed except more people. Even at that there were hang-ups once in awhile. Riggs was not unaware that someone was trying to throw a monkey wrench into the works. Probably Greer and his buddies, or someone like him. It didn't matter who it was, only that it was happening. Important supplies, but never *critical* ones, were often late in arriving. Like the cavalry in some Indian-surrounded fortress, someone was trying to cut them off. He was getting a lot of pressure to evacuate the station, send everybody back to Earth. He realized most of that pressure was political; that option had never been seriously considered by the scientists. It was far too risky. He had made his decision and he'd stick with it. No one came to the station, no one left. Everybody, including himself, was expendable.

A soft buzzer rang twice. Riggs automatically looked up at the clock. That would be Rob McGreggor with his afternoon update. He flipped on the monitor and Rob's upper body filled the screen. Fifteen feet away, yet separated by a steel bulkhead. Separated by more than that; age, the pressures of a lifetime of command, *responsibility*.

Rob looked haggard, everyone did. Too much tension, too little rest. He supposed he looked much the same. He did.

He nodded at Rob's cathode image.

"Some progress, Captain," said Rob. "On the oxygen tolerance experiment. We might have an angle there."

"How?"

"The exposed organism can't survive exposure to 100% oxygen. Anything up to 80% won't hurt them at all, they just become dormant. We get an LD50 at 95% and—."

"What's an LD50?"

"That means that exposure to 95% oxygen kills half of them; a lethal dose to half the population. One hundred percent kills them all—the exposed ones, that is. The internal ones aren't affected, as far as we can tell."

"How does that help us?"

"I'm getting to that. We've known all along that people working in the chamber didn't have an infection rate nearly as high as would be expected. Everybody else working with the patients, no matter what precautions are taken, end up with a very high incidence of infection. It follows that the high oxygen percentage used in the chamber keeps the transfer of the disease down. The additional pressure can only help, too."

"I'm sure the people who work in the chamber will be glad to hear that, but I fail to see how it's going to do the rest of us any good."

Rob took a deep breath. "The whole station could be made into a chamber."

"What?"

"If we had 100% oxygen as an atmosphere in the station, the organism wouldn't be able to exist outside the body. Avoid direct contact and we'd be able to contain the organism. We could at least hold our own that way."

"No," Riggs said thoughtfully. "It's impossible. This board, for instance, could never be made spark-proof. If a bulb went, the whole station would blow. And the laboratories . . . no, it couldn't be done."

"How about just part of the station, then? We could move most of the people in, run up the pressure a little. Pure oxygen. It would work."

Riggs stroked his chin, considered the proposal. It was feasible, but complicated. The risks were high; explosion, fire. Still, the way they were going, every day was a risk. Damn it, it was worth a shot.

"It might be possible," said Riggs. "It would be a big step, but it might work. The wards and nursing quarters, along with the operating rooms, are already equipped with sparkproof wiring because of the oxygen they routinely use there. We could include the adjacent sleeping quarters, seal the whole area off. That should give us enough room. Personnel will have to remove all metal artifacts; rings, watches, metal belt buckles. All electrical connections must be absolutely sparkproof or rendered inoperative. Normal atmosphere will have to be maintained through the rest of the station—I *must* stay at the board, others have similar responsibilities. Lord knows what Ground Control will say. But this is my command, my responsibility."

"It would buy us some time," said Rob.

"We could use a little bit of that," said Riggs. "I'll get the wheels in motion. I don't suppose you've come up with anything else."

"Afraid not."

"Keep at it."

"Thank you, Captain." Riggs cut off the connection.

The additional oxygen required wouldn't be too much of a problem. There was enough on board to initiate the procedure and Ground Control would undoubtedly send more, even if they didn't agree with the decision.

Riggs started on a checklist of things he would have to do to seal off part of the station. He buzzed for Sam, the chief engineer. He'd have to call Control. So many things. Too many decisions, too little rest. He wondered if he'd made the big mistake yet. The chance of explosion? The refusal of additional personnel? His determination not to evacuate the station? He rubbed his forehead. Too little rest.

Dr. Carlos Mendoza had been born in Sierra Mojada, Mexico. His parents had been poor and uneducated, lost in the shuffle that was modern-day Mexico. While the rest of the country was pulling itself from an agrarian way of life into an industrial society, Carlos' parents, like so many others, stayed in the shadows, stuck to the old ways.

While his parents worked in the fields, Carlos was taught by his grandparents. They had little use for books. What the young boy learned was a mixture of superstition and half-truths. His grandmother believed she could foretell the future, his grandfather was subject to fits, during which he would talk with all the great leaders of the past. Carlos was eleven years old before the state school system caught up with him. When placed in a decent environment he learned fast and well. Still, though he would never admit it, the memory of his grandparents was never far from the surface and at nights he would sometimes wake with dreams of his grandfather rolling on hard clay floors and his grandmother digging through the entrails of a freshly slaughtered chicken. He carried the ghosts of his past around with him like concrete blocks tied to the shoulders of his soul.

Carlos ran back the videotape of the snowball,

studied the printout of the monitors for that time period. Seven hours ago. There didn't seem to be anything unusual on the tape.

Research on all the alien creatures except the mantas had slowed to a near halt. About all that was being done now was observation and a few simple experiments. That was as it should be, he thought. Too bad it had taken such a traumatic incident to prove him right, but he had warned them. Still they didn't admit the error of their ways; it had been an accident. It was always an accident.

He flipped the pages of the printout. Nothing. He wasn't really sure what he was looking for. Maybe a sign of increased activity. Maybe nothing at all. He was sure he had the right time period. Seven hours ago he had been asleep. He'd dreamed of the snowball. He'd woken up shivering. It had seemed real to him.

It had seemed *very* real.

Sam hated to call the captain back. He wouldn't like this at all. He buzzed the board room.

"Yes Sam, what is it?" asked Riggs. "How does it look?"

"Most of it looks okay. It shouldn't be too hard. That's the oldest part of the station, it was occupied before the rest was completed. It was built as a separate unit and it isn't much trouble to refit the air locks. The big problem, though, is in the room next to the nursing quarters."

"What kind of a problem?"

"The main power relays there aren't sparkproof, never were. They're those new kinds, nothing I can do with them, can't bypass them or anything."

"We'll have to get them to ship us up some of the other kind, then."

Sam shook his head. "Sorry. Tried that. It's a special type, they don't make them any more, not sparkproof anyway. Only made a few of those to begin with. Said it would take a month to get one up here that would work in 100% oxygen."

"We don't have a month."

"I know that. They know that, too. You can try yelling at them if you want. I did, but I didn't get anywhere."

"Damn fools."

"I think there might be an alternative, Captain."

"What's that?"

"We had the same kind of relays on Gamma II. Close enough, anyway, that I could rig them up. According to the manifests, they weren't taken off for any of the Delta stations. Ought to still be there."

"Get somebody ready to take over for you, Sam. I'll have Ed run you over. We'll lick this yet."

"Sure thing, Captain," said Sam. Riggs faded from the screen as he cut off.

Sam was glad he wasn't in the captain's shoes. Machinery he could handle, but all this other stuff was beyond him. It all reduced itself to nuts and bolts, wire and tubes to Sam. That way he could get a handle on it. He didn't understand viruses and things like that. They were some kind of bugs or something.

Ed Brown had been his commander on Gamma II. It would be like going home again. Sort of.

Chapter Six

When Linda's shadows came, they came at night
on large black wings. Wings that beat the air with
thick, leathery slaps and drove away her personal
demons and replaced them with demons of a different cloth. Strange ones they were, with the touch
of terror and the taste of desperation. Images blurred
and shifted, nothing was clear, everything was seen
through a haze of silky gauze. The double darkness
of mountains against a clear black night. A breeze. A
shifting of lace curtains in a long-forgotten bedroom
in Oklahoma. Summer. No, fall; it's cool. The
familiar overlaid by the strange. Mountains. Twin
moons. A wheatfield golden in the afternoon sun, a
rusting pump with a creaky handle that gave forth
sparkling water so cold it hurt your teeth and
somewhere the mountains, the moons and a sweeping
horror out of the sky. Endless deserts, constant
hunger. The slap of leather, the creak of bones. And
there, over the mountains, a gentle humming, a buzz,

louder yet and the mountains slide away as the leather wings beat into the distance, fading into darkness until all that is left is the buzz.

Linda pushed back the sheets and turned off the alarm. She hated alarms, but lately she'd been forced into using one. All the staggered hours and weird shifts she'd been working had fouled up her sleeping patterns. She stretched, scratched herself. Something about a dream she'd been having brushed across her mind, flew away. She hadn't been sleeping well, bad dreams and everything. Tension, must be tension. She reached for the robe draped over the chair beside her bed. Her head ached.

At the sink in her room, she splashed cold water on her face, considered taking a shower, decided that she didn't have time. She ran a brush through her hair. It snagged on a tangle. Needed washing. Looks terrible. Put that off, too. Later. Maybe tomorrow, the next day. Whenever. She stepped into her slippers and went down the hall to the bathroom. Another day. Yawn.

Linda picked up a cup of tea in the cafeteria on her way to her first appointment. It tasted terrible. But it was hot and full of caffeine. If nothing else, it would keep her awake. She mixed in two packets of sugar and capped it, carrying it back to her office. Time to put on her official face. Ugh.

Candy was waiting when she arrived, a small pile of tracings on the desk. Yesterday's consults.

"You were right about Malcolm. Here, look." Candy spread out one of the tracings, flipped through the pages until she came to a section that had a lot of red marks along the margin. Parts of the record were circled, arrows were drawn to other sections. "Dr. Byrd read this one yesterday afternoon.

He confirmed encephalopathy. Look at the slowing in the temporal lobes; theta, delta. It's barely there, though. I couldn't be sure while I was running it. How'd you catch it?''

Linda uncapped her tea, sipped at it. "He came in yesterday for a routine update, seemed a little distracted, confused. Mostly he seemed to be just tired, but I decided to check, anyway. I ran him through one of our test sequences. He did okay except on the memory-recall section. He really blew that one. I looked back to his pre-tour scores and he'd been 100% right across the board. Something was wrong, but it was pretty selective.''

"You thought he might have been infected?"

"It was possible. Could have been a thousand other things, too. I sent him to you on the chance something might show up."

"It did. We hospitalized him right away."

"How's he doing?"

"Had a seizure last night. Going down fast."

Linda shook her head. "Wish we could have caught it sooner."

"I don't know that it would have helped," said Candy. "They're doing everything they can. Nothing seems to help very much."

"Still, if we were able to catch them early enough, it seems like there ought to be something they could do."

"I don't know what."

"Something's bound to turn up," said Linda. "What else do you have for me?"

"Nothing much. A couple possibles, nothing definite. Couldn't come up with anything on Paul. They took him off duty anyway, put him under rest and sedation. Strain, they said. Oh, have you seen Ted Shield lately?''

"No. Should I?''

"Could be. I ran him yesterday. Seemed a little slow in responding. Ran a nerve conduction on him, but it came up normal. I have a funny feeling about him, though. Nothing I can pin down. If you could work him in sometime soon, I'd appreciate it. Just as a favor. It's nothing official, just checking. Sometimes when I talk to them while I'm running the test, I can almost get as much information as I do off the paper."

"Be glad to, but not this afternoon," said Linda. "I'm going to be out on the wards. If I can find him, I'll try to slip him in this morning. If not, tomorrow for sure."

"I'd appreciate that."

"No problem."

"Thanks." Candy collected all her tracings, headed for the door. She started to say something about Paul, but decided not to bother Linda. It was pretty subjective: he'd really seemed sincere in his belief that he could see inside the mantas' minds. Ah well, it could wait. As she left, she passed Carlos Mendoza. He was on his way in to see Linda.

"Good morning, Carlos," said Linda. "Feeling better?"

"Yes, thank you. Dr. Topper gave me some pills." He sat in the chair in front of her desk. "They help me to sleep."

"Good. And the nightmares?"

"Gone. I no longer dream of ice and snow. Now when I sleep I have no dreams at all. Or if I do, I do not remember them and they do not bother me."

"Fine, Carlos." Linda reached into her desk drawer, pulled out a folder. "Here. I'd like you to fill out this form, answer these questions."

He looked at the papers. "What is this?" he said. "More nonsense? I filled these out the last time I was in here."

"These are different, Carlos. You know that all of us up here are guinea pigs. Just like those animals of yours. You poke the animals and I poke the people. It's just your turn to get poked, that's all."

"Hope this won't take long. I'm a very busy man," he grumbled, taking out a pen and starting to write.

Linda settled back and finished her tea, grown cold. Awful stuff. She closed her eyes and rested while Carlos wrote. She felt a vague uneasiness, or impatience. Running a slight fever this morning. A headache. Always too much to do. She would have had someone else give Carlos the tests, but she didn't have anyone else she could trust now. There were so many things involved, things that didn't show up on the forms. Some subjective, some the result of years of observation. A timer rang.

"Let me have that paper, Carlos," she said, leaning forward.

"But I'm not finished."

Not supposed to finish. Induce anxiety in the subject. Anger? Correlate second-page answers with the first.

"Never mind," she said. "Here's another sheet. Please try to answer as many as you can." This time she made a show of setting the timer, placing it on her desk in such a way that he couldn't see the face. It was all part of the routine. Carlos frowned, went back to his test.

She glanced at the paper he had handed her. His handwriting was sloppy, it slanted left for awhile, then right. She leafed through his folder to one of his earlier tests. Handwriting neat, precise. Maybe something, maybe not.

Linda found she was tapping her pencil against the desk top, stopped as soon as she realized she was doing it. Her foot was swinging back and forth, she shifted in her chair, put both feet on the floor. She felt nervous, anxious. That wasn't right. *He* was the one who was supposed to be anxious. It was all part of the test. Maybe it was the tea. Caffeine can produce symptoms of anxiety, even induce anxiety attacks. But one cup? It didn't seem likely.

"It's cold in here," said Carlos. "Can't you do anything about that?" He went back to writing.

Cold? No it couldn't be. All the offices in the station were kept at a constant temperature, supposedly a steady 22°C. Supposedly. She shivered. Couldn't be cold. Seemed a little bit, though. She was irritated. Why can't they keep the temperature right? With so many other things to deal with, we could at least be comfortable. She crossed her legs, started swinging her foot again. When the timer rang it startled her as much as it did Carlos.

"That's all," said Linda, taking his paper and slipping it into the folder. "How's your work coming along?"

He shrugged his shoulders. "Slow. There is much work to do and most are concentrating on the manta problem."

"Wouldn't you rather be doing that, too?"

"No, I guess not. There is much to be learned about the other animals. If we have to abandon the station, as some have said, they will die. All the information I can collect is valuable. I am of more use directing what little research we can carry out under the conditions. It is important work and may yet turn out to be the more valuable in the long run.''

This was a complete reversal from their last conversation. At that time, Carlos had been angry and resentful that Rob had been chosen to head the investigation. She knew that Rob had offered him a position working on the manta problem and that he had turned it down in spite. Had he really adjusted to the situation or was there something else? A personality change? Psychological or physiological? Was it the medication he was taking? Almost anything was possible. It would take more tests to find out.

"Are you still working with the dragonfish?" she asked.

"A little. Mostly I've been concentrating on the snowball.''

A cold breeze seemed to slide through the room. They both shivered. *Transference*, she thought, and shook her head as if to clear it. I think I feel what he feels. It comes from identifying too closely with your patients. I'm slipping. Usually more objective than this. Slight fever, not feeling too good. Resistance down. All sorts of things. Everybody feels rotten. Keep him talking. Personality change.

"Are you getting anywhere?" she asked.

She was feeling a little dizzy. It seemed hot in the room. Or maybe cold.

"Not really," he said. "Accumulating data, that's about all.''

Linda felt very spacy, drawn out. Carlos seemed to take such a long time between words. Her head hurt. She pressed her forehead, *warm*, and squeezed the bridge of her nose. Concentrate. It wasn't cold in the room, in fact, it seemed too hot to her. Something was wrong.

"No more nightmares, right?" she asked. "The dragonfish you were dreaming about are leaving you alone now?" *Got to keep objective.*

"That's right," he said. "No dragonfish, no snowballs. I sleep like a baby."

Snowballs? He hadn't mentioned snowballs before. Is he telling the truth? Or is he saying what he thinks I want to hear? There was a time I could have been able to tell in an instant, without hesitation. We're all tired, overworked. Can't take any chances.

She filled out a form, tore the top sheet from the pad.

"Take this to Candy," she said. "Have her set up an appointment as soon as possible."

He looked at her sharply.

Defensive, she thought. Why do *I* feel defensive?

"What's this?" he said. "More needles? Is she going to stick those wires in my head again?"

A twinge of fear. Did I feel that? she thought. From where? From him? From me?

"I'm very busy," he said.

"It'll only take a few minutes. Look at it as collecting data. Like your snowballs."

Again a wave of cold air.

Carlos grumbled and left. Linda felt an immediate sense of relief. He seemed to take the cold air with him.

Calmer now, Linda sat back and looked at the forms. Handwriting *was* a lot sloppier. She paid particular attention to the sections on logic. They seemed loose, somehow. He should be very strong there. She walked around the desk and pulled his entire file. Better run the whole thing through the computer.

Two hours later, Linda dropped off the forms to be processed at the computer center. Ray told her it would be a while before they could get at them. Things were really busy, all the trunk lines were filled.

It was still too early for Linda's shift on the wards, so she decided to walk over to the aliens' sector. Maybe Carlos would be there and she could get some idea of the work he was doing.

Carlos wasn't around and the area was deserted, except for Alan Brand, a technician, who dozed lightly in front of the monitors. It was the snowball's dark period and there wasn't any activity to speak of. Alan nodded at Linda's approach and then closed his eyes. The monitors were being taped, so his presence wasn't actually required, not during the night periods. As Linda took a seat, he slid down in his chair, rested his head on his arms.

Linda yawned. She hadn't realized how tired she felt.

It had been years ago. Sometimes it felt like yesterday.

Linda had spent a month by herself in a rented cabin on the Gulf of Mexico. It was just before she started her internship. Rob had wanted to come along, but she had asked him not to. She was nice about it, but firm. No, there wasn't anybody else. She just wanted to be alone, think some things through. He didn't press her.

The cabin was weathered cedar, raised up on cinder blocks. There was a large screen porch across the front and a small room on top. It had no electricity or running water. The water from the pump was too salty to drink, so she had to truck her cooking and drinking water in from a spring about ten miles away. Her nearest neighbor was twice that distance. The rent was sixty dollars.

The day she moved in was hot and quiet. There had been a lot to do, not much time to look around before dark. At night the noises startled her. Not noises, really; sounds, night sounds. Thousands of frogs, all talking at once. Crickets. The soft hoot of an owl in the pine trees. The grunt of an old alligator somewhere off in the marsh. Night birds with night songs. She sat on the porch in an old rocking chair. One arm of the chair was loose, the floor creaked underneath her. Lazy clouds drifted across a full moon. A tree frog, glistening green, crawled up the screen in front of her. She fell asleep on the porch, gently rocking back and forth. When she woke, the sun was just beginning to burn off the morning fog.

Days went like that, stretched into nights. Long nights, quiet nights. She missed Rob. Often at night she would sit by the flickering orange light of the kerosene lamp and write him long letters. In the morning she would look at the letters and feel embarrassed. A grown woman, writing sentimental stuff like that. With mixed feelings, she would stuff the letters in the wood-burning stove and use them to help heat her morning coffee. It was forty miles to the nearest post office, anyway.

Chopping wood for the stove made her feel good. There was a large stack of old wood that had to be split and chopped down before it would fit in the stove. The first time she did it, she swung the ax until her arms ached and her t-shirt was drenched with sweat. Then she realized there was no one for miles, so she took off her shirt, hung it on a tree limb and worked until she was ready to drop. She had done quite a bit, more than she had expected. Her hands were covered with blisters. She looked at the pile of wood and smiled. What had started as a large stack of big logs and stumps was now stove-size pieces. There was something very satisfying about doing a job and seeing the direct result of your labor. She wondered how many people in the world got that kind of satisfaction. Did construction workers go back later to look at a wall they had built, a roof they had helped put up? She thought maybe they did. She hoped so. She felt proud and strong and walked the winding path through the edge of the marsh to a small piece of sandy beach where she stripped off her shorts and swam in the crystal water, feeling good, splashing and singing out of the pure joy of being alive. She fell asleep on the sand and woke only as the sun was setting, an orange ball that hung on the edge of the gulf painting the world with an impossible splash of pastels. As she walked back to the cabin it got dark and the wind died down. The mosquitos ate her alive. She didn't care.

Linda indulged herself. If she felt like being lazy, then, by God, she'd be lazy. Some days she worked hard, other days she just sat around. She finished the research paper she'd been working on. In the quiet, she realized that she had never been this alone before. Even though she'd been on her own for years, there'd always been someone else around. Mother, father, Rob, neighbors, friends; someone was almost always nearby. Here, if she dropped a sweatshirt on the floor or left a coffee cup sitting next to the bed, it would stay there until she moved it. Nobody was around to change anything but herself. She liked it, and at the same time it frightened her. One night a small raccoon climbed to the top of the porch steps. She fed it some scraps and it came back every night after that, an hour after sunset, nervous at first, bolder later on. She found herself waiting for it and talking to it when it finally came. It never stayed long enough.

She had her favorite places. One was an old gnarled tree on the edge of the marsh. It had been dead for years, but wouldn't give up the fight. Its old roots dug deep into the ground and had held it against winds, tides, and hurricanes. Its bare branches were thick and strong. She liked to sit out on one special limb over the water and rest her back against its trunk. The water was a gentle lapping at the base of the tree, the marsh stretched out before her, gradually giving way to the open water beyond. The marsh was full of birds; ducks, herons, egrets, hawks. Mullet spashed in the water. Pelicans flew over the gulf, reminding her of other pelicans, other times. She couldn't remember the problems she had come out here to solve. They had faded away, back onto the great mass of things that didn't really matter, things that weren't really important. Maybe she had solved them, maybe they had just slipped back into perspective. She heard a car door slam. It took a minute to place the sound. She hadn't heard a car or seen another human face for three weeks. She walked back to the cabin.

There was a car pulled into the front yard. It was dusty from the long gravel road to the cabin. It had

local tags on it, rental plates. She walked up to the
porch and Rob was standing there. He looked embarrassed.

"I'll leave," he said. "All you have to do is tell me
and I'll go. I just wanted to see you."

Linda threw her arms around him, hugged him
tight.

"Come on, silly," she said with an easy laugh.
"I've got so much to show you."

The hallway was dimly lit. A lone figure walked
with a preoccupied air through the semidarkness.
From all outward signs he looked calm. Inside he was
a raging turmoil:

*Fools, all of them. Damn fools. They have eyes,
but they're blind. They have ears, yet they're deaf.
They can't see or hear the things I have knowledge
of. I alone am spoken to by the voices from the stars.
I alone am chosen.*

*It is like the tales of my mother's mother. The tea
leaves and the steaming entrails were partly right.
The computers and the microscopes were partly
wrong. I know; I can hear them, they talk to me. The
old legends come true; they have arrived from the
stars to lead us. We must follow them. My father
believed in devils. I scoffed, yet parts of me believed,
too. There have alwyas been shadows in my life that
could not be explained. All my life I have been
groomed for this position. I will lead my people, all
people, from the shadows to the clear, cold light of
the stars.*

The figure paused at an intersection in the hallway.
He rocked back and forth slightly, hands clenching
and unclenching. Two voices drifted up from the

corridor to his right. He turned to his left, away from them.

Cold. So very cold. Through the unimaginable darkness they have reached me. They seek me out—me—the chosen one.

Even yet there are doubts, suspicions. I can't be sure if the uncertainty lives with them or inside myself. I have to be proven worthy. There must be tests. I must be pure. Pure.

I feel another approaching. How clear it is. He is not pure. He suspects nothing, knows nothing. He is as deaf and blind as the others. In his mind I see blood and sharp instruments. Blood. He is not pure.

Dr. Mellon was taking the long way back from the wards, wandering around the deserted corridors on the far side of the station. This area of half-completed rooms and exposed gridwork would eventually become research quarters, expanded medical facilities. Delta III was designed to grow as funds and needs increased. Hopefully it wouldn't become as obsolete as the other stations had. Dr. Mellon liked to walk, especially where there was little chance of interruption. This was an ideal place.

As he walked, his mind wandered, skipped: the operation he'd performed that morning, a crisp, cold afternoon walking across the campus of the University of Oklahoma, his first day of internship at Johns Hopkins, yesterday's lunch, special patients with special problems he'd have to deal with this afternoon on rounds, somewhere a woman darted in and out of his thoughts; blue eyes and sandy brown hair scattered across a pillow so long ago. So long ago.

In short, Dr. Mellon was thinking of everything

and nothing at all. He didn't see the shadow figure crouched in the doorway, a short piece of metal pipe gripped tightly in his hand.

You are not pure. By fire and ice, you must be cleansed. You who live by blood must die by blood. I alone am worthy. This is my test and I must not, will not, fail. In the coldness of death will come your purity, the purity of ice. Now!

The shadow moved, a blur in the corner of Dr. Mellon's eye. An automatic reflex drew his arms up before he could register anything else. Then he saw it was a man. He was confused, the pieces didn't fit. Had he seen service, he would have reacted at once. But his training was in the healing arts and what he was seeing didn't fit any pattern he was familiar with. An instant later he integrated "man" with a face, a body. He recognized the face, but the actions were confusing. It was all happening too fast. In the space of 1.3 seconds, Dr. Mellon ran a gamut of reactions: startle, confusion, recognition, annoyance, and finally fear. He was slow. Too slow.

Now! The evil in your body must be driven out. Could they speak with tongues, they would tell me to do this. You recognize me. See this face, know that I speak for those from the stars.

The first blow caught Dr. Mellon along the side of his head in an area he would have described as the anterior temporal bone. It was a heavy pipe. He went down, hard. He was dead before he hit the floor.

But that didn't stop his attacker, who swung the pipe wildly in a sweeping arc again and again on the prostrate form. He swung until the bloody pipe slipped from his hands and crashed down the hall. Even that didn't stop him as he continued to beat on the lifeless body.

Now it is done. I have purged the evil from your body. I alone am pure, the chosen one. Through me you will speak . . . speak . . . speak. . . .

The pounding stopped. The man stood, bewildered, shaking his head. Methodically he dragged the body into one of the unfinished rooms, covered it with a stack of loose cardboard. He walked down the hall, found the bloody pipe, wiped it with a rag, took it with him. He continued around the back way, taking a sharp turn that would lead him to where the alien animals were kept.

It was cold. Strange stars drifted overhead, the moon was too close, or was it too far? Such bitter cold. A ball, the primal fetal position, conserving as much warmth as possible. It was a deep rest, more than sleep, a death of sorts. A nightly dying in order to live one more day as soon the sun would break the distant horizon, bringing fitful life, a chance to feed, a chance at one more day.

Linda shivered, stretched her arms. Half asleep, she felt like she was torn between two places. A part of her, fading even as she tried to catch her thoughts, seemed to be in another plane of existence. She tried to grab it, analyze it. It slipped away. A dream, most likely. She'd been dozing.

Alan was asleep at the monitor, his head on the desk. The lights had been turned down. Yawning, Linda hooked her feet under the chair in front of her. The monitor was a dim square above the sleeping man.

The scene on the monitor hadn't changed while she'd been asleep. The faint outline of the snowball could barely be seen in the dim illumination of its induced nighttime. It was folded up, a ball covered with a thin layer of ice. Motionless, waiting for the artificial sun to rise, providing warmth, nutrients, life.

Linda glanced at the digital on the wall, soft red numbers shifting noiselessly. She must have been asleep longer than she realized, it was late. She'd have to hurry to get to the wards in time for her shift. She rose quietly, so as not to wake the sleeping man. On her way out, she pressed the palm of her hand against the wall of the snowball's enclosure. It felt cold to the touch, but she knew that she must be imagining it. These walls were fully insulated. Still she shivered, and as she walked away she felt a vague longing for the warmth of an unknown sun.

The man stood in the shadows and watched Linda leave. He would attend to her later—she was special. But first he had a job to do.

He left the darkness of the back of the room and quietly approached Alan asleep in front of the monitor. He stood for a moment behind the man, watching the screen with an almost hypnotic intensity.

Sleeping. Cold. Purity. The rest of ice to recharge the soul. Rebirth. We must all be reborn. Evil will be driven from the Earth and we shall inherit the stars. Evil.

He grabbed the sleeping man by the hair, pulled his head back, and slammed it down against the metal desk. The man had no time to react. He did it several times and when he was convinced that the man was dead, he relaxed his grip and let the body slide to the floor.

Unhurriedly, he walked to the dressing station at the side of the room and stripped his clothes off, dropped them in the recycler. He washed and got a nondescript pair of scrubs off the shelf. Almost as an afterthought, he dragged the body across the room and stuffed it into an empty locker.

Linda washed up and stepped into a fresh set of scrubs. She was late and didn't like it. It wasn't part of her nature to be late and in her rush she almost put her regular shoes back on instead of the static-free slippers. Damn. Be forgetting to screw her head on straight next.

She went up to the desk. Susan was holding down the fort. She looked ragged, but so did everybody else.

"Good to see you," said Susan, wiping an errant strand of hair away from her face. "I thought maybe you'd gotten tied up."

"Just can't seem to get myself together today, that's all," said Linda.

"You're not the only one. This place is a mess. Shirley and Troy haven't shown up yet and I can't reach Dr. Mellon. He's due on rounds and he isn't answering his page."

Linda nodded. It was like that all over the station. "Who do I have today?" she asked.

"I'd like you to cover the blue wing with Marlene. She's got the charts. That's the med tray, there."

Linda picked up the blue plastic tray and started to walk away when the silence of the nursing station was broken by the urgent crackle of the public address system.

"Red blanket, section L-47, team alpha. Attention team alpha, there is a red blanket, section L-47."

Susan pressed a button on her intercom and spoke rapidly into it for a few seconds. "Come on," she yelled to Linda as she jumped from the raised nursing podium. "We might need you." She grabbed a red tray and headed for the door. As they entered the hallway they were met by Dr. Sheldon, who was filling in for Dr. Mellon as team physician for alpha. Dr. Sheldon was an anesthesiologist, not a surgeon, but that didn't matter much. He was a doctor and the rules said that each emergency medical team had to have a doctor. They were lucky they weren't down to veterinarians yet.

Section L-47 was in the research sector, the area where the snowball was kept, the area Linda had just left. This fact didn't escape her attention.

"Accident?" she asked as they ran through the hall.

"Don't know," said Susan. "Multiple injuries is all they said."

They rounded the corner and pushed through the doors into the snowball's viewing area. The lights had been turned back to full bright. A group of people were clustered around a prostrate form stretched out in front of the lockers. They stood to one side to let the medical team through. Alan Brand. It looked bad.

Susan and Dr. Sheldon knelt at Alan's head, loosening his shirt and probing his mouth.

"Airway's blocked," said Susan.

Dr. Sheldon nodded, grabbed an esophageal obturator from the emergency tray, removed it from its plastic wrapper, attempted to insert it through Alan's mouth. Linda had her hand on Alan's neck.

"Heart's weak, but steady," she said.

"Strip him," said Susan, handing Linda a pair of scissors. "God, something really got to him," she added, talking to herself.

Linda slit Alan's shirt up the side with a few quick motions. Before she had finished, Susan was pushing it aside and attaching the EKG leads.

"Start an IV," said Dr. Sheldon, still working with the tube. "Straight Ringers, full drip. He's lost a lot of blood."

Linda pulled a butterfly out of the box and inserted the needle into Alan's vein. As soon as it started to flow, she handed the bottle of Ringers to a bystander to hold.

Susan was holding a small strip of paper as it came out of the portable EKG. "He's throwing PVC's," she said. "Rate's dropping."

"There," said Dr. Sheldon. "I've got it. Bag him."

Susan slipped the green rubber bag over the tube curling out of Alan's mouth and started squeezing it, forcing air into Alan's lungs.

Dr. Sheldon moved around to the portable EKG machine that sat on the floor next to the emergency tray. It was about the size of a cigar box, and he took the EKG strip in his hand as the machine spit it out.

"Shit," said Dr. Sheldon. "There he goes. Flat."

He pounded once on Alan's chest, leaned back to check the EKG strip for results. Nothing. A straight black line kept coming out.

"Goddamn it," he said, straddling Alan, starting the rythmic compression of closed chest massage. He kept it up for about thirty seconds, then stopped to check the EKG. Still flat. He continued the massage for another thirty seconds and checked again. Nothing.

"Two amps bicarb," he said and continued the closed chest massage.

Linda handed the two prefilled syringes to Susan,

ripping them from their prepack. Susan injected them into the IV line.

"Where the hell's that goddamn cart?" she mumbled to herself.

As if in answer, the door swung open and two men rolled in a metal cart, pad on top, emergency equipment underneath.

"Sorry we're late, but—."

"Cut it. The paddles. Quick."

One of the men passed a pair of paddles to Dr. Sheldon. They were about half the size of ping-pong paddles and connected to a machine underneath the cart by a pair of thick, coiled wires. The other man fiddled with some switches until a green light glowed on the machine.

"Ready, Doctor," he said.

"Clear," said Dr. Sheldon. Linda and Susan backed away. He placed one paddle over Alan's heart and the other on the side of his rib cage. "Now!" He squeezed the handles on the paddles and Alan jerked, arms and legs giving one solid twitch and relaxing.

"Still flat," said Susan, watching the strip unfold as Dr. Sheldon paused.

"Again," he said. "Now." Once more Alan's body convulsed in a massive spasm.

"Hey." said Susan. "We're getting something."

Dr. Sheldon bent over to look at the tape. A blip, two. He held his breath. Another. Then the heart seemed to kick in on its own. A rhythm started; irregular, faint, but there nonetheless. Linda started pumping the bag again.

"Move him," said Dr. Sheldon. "Oxygen first. Hook him up."

The men fitted a flexible hose where the bag had

been attached. Underneath the cart the oxygen supply hissed softly.

Alan started thrashing around, waving his arms, kicking his legs. It didn't mean that he was gaining consciousness, only that his body was reacting to the oxygen deprivation. It made him harder to handle, though. It took all five of them to get him strapped on top of the cart.

"Take him," said Dr. Sheldon, and as the two men disappeared with the cart, he turned to Susan. "Who's in the ER?" he asked.

"Dawson ought to be there by now," she said.

"I'd better go," he said. "They might need help." He started to follow the cart, stopped by the door, turned around. "Hey, Susan," he said. "Thanks. You too, Linda."

"Good job," said Susan.

"I don't know," he said. "Don't think we got to him in time." He went out the door and down the hall.

"He's pretty good," said Susan, picking up the scattered remnants of the emergency tray. "Most of the specialists we get up here have their noses so far up in the air that they can't handle anything like this."

Linda didn't hear her. She was staring back to the chairs where she had been sitting. It had been Alan instead of her. There couldn't have been more than a couple of minutes difference. It could have been her. Why? Who?

"Hey, Linda," said Susan. "What's with you?"

"I don't know," said Linda. "I just don't know." Then she shivered. It wasn't cold.

Riggs looked at Dr. Dawson in the viewscreen. She

looked terrible, fatigue etched hard lines in her face.
It had been a long operation. "What do you think his
chances are?" he asked.

"Realistically? None, I'd say. Close to zero.
Massive brain damage. In my opinion, I doubt he'll
ever regain consciousness. We may have saved his life
for now, but that's about all."

"If he does come around, let me know," said
Riggs. "I'll have Bounds of security send someone
around to sit with him. We've got to find out what
happened."

Evelyn Dawson shrugged. "I don't think it will
help. Even if by some miracle he should come around
long enough to say anything—assuming he has
enough brain left to talk with, which I doubt—he
probably won't have anything to say that would help
you. People usually blank out trauma like that. Can't
remember anything about it."

"It's worth a try. I'll have someone over there
shortly."

"Suit yourself. I think it's a waste of time."

Riggs cut the connection. Dawson was probably
right. Bounds had said there were no signs that Alan
had fought back at all. Must have caught him off
guard or something. Probably wouldn't remember a
thing. Still, they had to try.

He thumbed a switch open, spoke into his
microphone. "Get me McGreggor," he said.

"Yes, sir."

A few moments later, Riggs' screen chimed and
Rob's face appeared in front of him.

"Good evening, Captain."

"I doubt that, Rob. I guess you've heard."

"About Alan Brand? There's been some talk.
Somebody said he'd been attacked."

"That's right," sighed Riggs. "But there's more."
Oh damn it, was there more.

"I don't understand."

"Dr. Mellon. . . . "

"Lee?"

"They found him about ten minutes ago. He'd been dead for hours."

"Dead?"

"It appears he was clubbed to death."

"My God."

"What I want to know, Rob," asked Riggs, weighing his words very carefully, "is whether or not this, this disease thing or whatever it is . . . could it cause someone to crack up? Go crazy? Do something like this?"

Rob thought a second. "I suppose it's possible. The false thought patterns could be hard for someone to integrate, especially if they were the slightest bit unstable to begin with. The person experiencing the hallucinations probably can't differentiate them from the real thing."

"Could it cause violent behavior?"

"It could cause almost anything, sir."

Riggs shuddered. That's all they needed.

The artificial sun rose above the artificial horizon. Ice melted and the stone pinged in the thin air. The snowball didn't stir; not yet, even though it was slowly waking. Cold still chilled its body, its internal movements were minimal. Time enough yet, let the sun get a little higher. Cold. Just a faint hint of warmth to come. It could wait.

Under the monitor a man sat watching. He shivered, but only partially from the cold. He looked constantly over his shoulder, his fingers drummed a nervous tattoo on the desk top. He went through the motions of filling out the log, but his thoughts were someplace else. Fear drove dark slivers of ice into his heart. He wrapped his jacket tighter around him.

Chapter Seven

Ed Brown checked the cabin pressure in the small spacecraft for the fifth time. All lights were green. Sam sat next to him in the co-pilot's seat. Wayne Lewis, one of Sam's men, sat in the jump space behind the two seats.

"Delta III, this is Relay One. I've got a green board."

"Roger, Ed. You look real good from here. Just give me a count."

"Taking it in five. Mark."

"Got you. Houston, do you copy?"

"Roger, Delta III, this is Houston. We have you at four thirty-seven and counting. It's your baby. We'll just sit back and watch the show."

"Four minutes," said Brown.

"This is Delta III. Automatic sequence initiated. Give me a confirmation on battery bank Baker. We get a murky reading here."

Ed reached out in front of him and flipped a

plastic switch to three different positions. Then he leaned over in front of Sam and did the same with a switch on the co-pilot's side. "Baker is green," he said. "No fluctuations."

"Got it Ed. Hold it, message from the captain. He says not to drag your ass on this one."

"And I was planning to stop off for a beer."

"Sorry about that. Approaching T minus one. Mark. It's all yours, Ed. Good luck."

"Thanks."

Ed was busy for the next thirty seconds. Although the launch was mostly automatic, it was a procedure initially designed to be handled by a pilot and a co-pilot. A co-pilot was a luxury they couldn't afford.

"Main arms back. Twenty seconds."

All that was holding the craft to the station were two small breakaways attached by explosive bolts. At seven seconds, the bolts were fired.

"You're on your own, Relay One. Three . . . two. . . ."

"Ignition," said Brown and the small craft eased its way out of its pocket on the side of Delta III. Slowly it drifted far enough from the station for Ed to fire the main thrusters.

"Delta III, I need an update. I seem to have a small yaw here."

"That's right, Ed, we copy. Nothing to worry about, we've got it. The new numbers should be in your box now."

A flow of numbers raced across the screen in front of Brown. "Roger, Delta III, I have them now." He made small adjustments to correct for pitch and yaw, to line himself up properly. Gradually the two gridworks representing real and ideal lined up on the screen, a series of green numbers flashed to the right of the gridwork. "Do you copy that, Delta III?" he asked.

"Roger. We read a burst of 8.4 seconds at 65%. Looks good."

"Engines primed. Number one, check. Number two, check. Backup, check. Count of five . . . four . . . three. . . ." Brown held his hand over the manual override switch and only after the engines had fired on schedule and cut off did he relax.

"Nice burn, Relay One. Right on the button. All the numbers look good. Have a nice trip."

"Tell Riggs to hold down the fort," said Brown. "The cavalry is on the way."

Only then did Brown have the time and opportunity to see how his passengers were taking all this. Sam looked relaxed, but Wayne looked a little pale.

"What do you think?" asked Brown. "Just like sailing across Lake Placid, isn't it? A piece of cake."

Wayne looked like he was going to throw up.

Jodie finished a mouse, thought for a moment of green, rolling hills. Time had taken the edge off the memory, years had brought her here from there.

When she had been growing up on a small farm in central Kentucky, a space station was far from her mind. She could never imagine herself cooped up like that. She loved the outdoors, spent as much time as possible in the woods surrounding their home. Her other love was animals, wild or domesticated. Her family life had been uneven. Her mother, a humorless individual at the best of times, went through four bad marriages while Jodie was growing up. For any warmth in her life, she had the barn cats and, finally, a horse.

The horse was a large factor in her life. When she was fifteen and most of the girls in her group were moving from horses to boys, Jodie stuck with horses. One horse in particular, named Moses, bought with and maintained by her own money—money earned during afternoons at the drug store, weekends at the grocery. Moses was a beautiful horse; they had many golden afternoons. Then two years later that winter came and she held Moses' head in her lap in the snow and there was no money for a vet and she swore she'd never let a thing like that happen again. To anybody.

Jodie wanted to go to veterinary school, tried desperately to do it, but there wasn't enough money. She could have gotten a scholarship, but that would have meant leaving home and she was needed there. She drifted into a job at a local biological supply house, mixing solutions. They paid her way to night school at the nearby community college. Since they didn't offer veterinary science, she studied biology and chemistry. Much to her surprise, she discovered she had an aptitude for it. She liked it, was good at it, and when Operation Pegasus brought back the alien creatures, she had been working with Dr. Carlos Mendoza. When work began in earnest on Delta III, his grant application had been approved. When he went into space, he took her with him.

On Delta III she was a floating technician, working wherever she was needed the most. Now she was working for Rob. She often wondered what kind of a veterinarian she would have been.

She was tired, dead tired. Rob had left two hours ago to get some rest. He'd be back to spell her before too long. She wiped the sweat from her forehead and carefully loaded another syringe.

This particular line of research involved infecting

different kinds of experimental animals to see if any of them developed antibodies to the organism. So far all the results had been negative. Now they were trying some of Rob's sterile-raised mice. She didn't expect any better luck with these, but it was worth a chance. Anything was worth a chance. When things got bleak, Jodie always figured the best thing to do was to keep plugging along.

She reached into the plexiglass container and grabbed one of the mice with her gloved right hand. With the thumb and forefinger of her left hand she took it by the scruff of the neck, pinning its tail between the little finger of her left hand and her palm. This freed her right hand and gave her a firm grip on the mouse, belly up, with her left. She swabbed the mouse's belly with an alcohol-soaked cotton ball. Then she took a syringe and injected 0.10cc of fluid just under the mouse's skin. It left a small lump. It also left one of the organisms. She color-coded the mouse's tail with a marker and dropped it into a new container.

Carefully, again, she loaded another syringe.

She was cool at what she did, smoothly professional. It was dangerous, no doubt about it, but that seldom entered her mind. Working with dangerous substances was something she'd had lots of practice in. She had faith that if she was careful, she'd be safe.

Still, she was surrounded by flasks and vials filled with an organism they really knew very little about. It didn't worry her, but at the same time, she didn't forget it, either. The memory of the amino acid analyzer accident was too fresh in her mind.

Nor did she forget that a disease known as toxoplasmosis had once been as unknown as the one she was working on. It had been carried in the laboratory using mice in exactly the same way. At that time the segment of the population with the highest incidence of toxoplasmosis was laboratory technicians working with it.

She heard the door open.

"You're early, Rob. Thanks," she said without looking up. There was no answer, so she turned around. It wasn't Rob.

"You can't come in here dressed like that. This is a sterile room." Her first reaction was indignation. It was followed quickly by recognition, consternation and fear as the man quickly crossed the small room and pushed her up against the table.

Even as the bottles and vials crashed and slopped around her, her prime concern was for the experiments and the cultures. When she noticed the man was carrying a piece of pipe, she began to feel fear for her safety. By then it was too late.

Rob woke with a start. His intercom was buzzing, his head hurt.

"Yeah," he said wearily, fumbling with the controls. "Rob here."

Linda's face appeared on the screen. "There's been an accident, Rob. Jodie. In the culture rooms."

"What? Where?" Not there. No, not in the culture rooms. Oh, shit.

"It looks serious. You'd better get down there right away."

"I'm gone," he said, breaking the connection.

The hallway to the culture rooms was sealed off. Bounds of security stood by the door, blocking the way. It was a confused scene, there were a lot of people milling around. At first Bounds didn't want to let him through, but a quick call to Riggs straightened it out. There was likely to be infectious material loose in there and Rob should take a look around before the decontamination crew started work. Rob donned an isolation suit, got some help adjusting his mask, and went through the double set of doors into the corridor to the culture rooms.

It was strangely quiet on the other side of the doors. Down the hall he could hear muted voices and he followed them to the room where he and Jodie had been working.

He wasn't sure what he expected to find, but what he saw shocked him. Jodie looked terrible, there was blood everywhere. Two people in isolation garments were huddled over her, two others stood nearby. It took a second for Rob to realize that all the blood wasn't from Jodie—that most of it had come from the broken cultures.

"How is she?" he asked.

"It looks bad."

They strapped Jodie on a cart and started to roll her away. Rob looked at her as she went by. So pale. Her hair was matted with blood. How could such a thing happen?

One of the suited figures walked over to Rob. He could barely make out the features behind the mask. It was Dr. Woods. She was a surgical resident, had come up on the last shuttle before all this had happened.

"She's not going to make it, Rob."

He nodded quietly. Damn it all.

"We'll do what we can, but it isn't going to be enough."

"Thanks, June. I know you'll try," said Rob weakly.

"We'll do everything we can, it's just. . . . " she trailed off, made an ambiguous gesture with her hands, turned and followed the cart out the door.

Rob looked around the room. God, what a mess. He walked to the overturned table and picked up the log book. It was bloodsplattered, but complete up to the last entry, the one she must have been working on when she was attacked. Out of the corner of his eye, Rob saw a small mouse dart behind a cabinet. Bounds had told him not to disturb anything, just to check and see if the contamination could be contained.

Rob clenched his fists out of anger and a mounting sense of futility. Clean up the mess, pick up the goddamn pieces. What a crock of shit. How long can this hellfire go on? Jodie's dying, it would take days to straighten out this mess. Several experiments were surely ruined, cultures lost, everything. For what? Was it worth it? The killer, madman, whatever, was only part of the problem. So many other things. When Brown and Sam got back, some of the pressure would be off. It would buy some time. But time for what? To stumble around in the dark? To die a little more slowly? To remain trapped as surely as the mantas are trapped, the mice are trapped? Like the mice, we're all expendable, ready to be sacrificed for the common good. Or, like Jodie, for no reason at all. It didn't make any sense, none at all.

Rob sat down, tried to close his eyes to the mess. He sighed deeply, searching for some reason other than inertia to keep on going. When he opened his eyes, everything looked the same. Jodie was still dying, the mess was still there.

Gamma II spun slowly against the background of

stars, half the deserted station in glaring brightness, half in near-total darkness. It reminded Brown of some sort of a metallic skeleton, a half-dismembered memory of the station it used to be. Large sections of the station were missing, here and there portions of the outer shell had been removed, leaving exposed the internal gridwork of beams and struts. Many parts of the Gamma stations had been salvaged for use in building the Delta series, but the records showed the relays they needed should still be there.

"Quite a change," said Sam. "She doesn't look a bit like she used to."

"Seen better days, that's for sure," said Brown. Gamma II had been his command for awhile and although he didn't consider himself the emotional type, it still felt a little strange to be coming back this way. "Let's go in. Give me the numbers."

Brown made small thruster adjustments in response to the figures that Sam read off to him, figures provided by the onboard computer. Between burns, Brown looked out the window in front of him, getting a visual check of the results. It wasn't that he mistrusted the computer, but years of flying had taught him that there was something that the cold machines couldn't provide; a sense of feel, of *rightness*, the "seat-of-the-pants" *knowing* that the approach was correct. Everything looked good. Slowly the station stopped spinning in the window and then it was the stars that spun behind the seemingly motionless satellite. The board flashed green— their rotation matched that of the station.

"Here we go," said Brown.

Silently, the small ship moved slowly towards the station. From inside, there was no apparent motion. The station just seemed to loom larger and larger in front of them. Sam flinched a little and Brown could hear a sharp intake of breath from Wayne behind him. They stopped a scant five meters from the station's surface.

"Nice shot," said Sam.

"Thanks," said Brown, busy flipping switches in front of him. He stretched, snapped his helmet shut. "Time for our little walk, gentlemen. Switch to internal power."

Brown double-checked the tell-tales on their suits. Satisfied, he vented the cabin. Pushing himself from the pilot's seat, he half drifted, half pulled his way back to the hatch. Flipping up the protective covers from a pair of widely separated switches, he palmed the door open. He could hear Sam and Wayne's breath heavy in his ears as it was picked up by their microphones. It sounded like they were standing right behind him. He reached through the door and attached the tether to a ring clip on the outside of the ship. He snapped the other end of the tether to his suit and slowly eased himself out the hatch.

No matter how much time he'd spent in space, there was a special thrill about being outside that Brown never seemed to lose. He didn't need biosensors to tell that his heart and respiration levels were elevated. The Earth was a huge mottled globe hanging in space above his head, covered with swirling clouds. Brown had a brief attack of vertigo, a small spell of dizziness that quickly passed. It wasn't an unpleasant feeling.

"Everything okay, Ed?"

"Yeah, Sam, sure."

Brown came out of his moment of reverie. Back to business. He coiled the tether into loose loops, made sure there were no tangles. Scanning the surface of

the station opposite him, he picked a relatively unob-
structed place to land. Gently he pushed off the side
of the ship and drifted across to the station.

Jodie Pope lay in a bed in the intensive care unit,
barely alive. Tubes fed her, chemicals maintained her
metabolic balance, a respirator did her breathing for
her. She was heavily dosed with a synthetic curare to
keep her from fighting the respirator. Painkillers and
sedatives dripped into her arm along with carefully
mixed fluids. Everything was measured, weighed,
calculated to two decimal points. It was all aimed at
keeping her alive. Nobody figured she had a chance.
They were right about that.

They also figured that she couldn't hear, couldn't
understand what was happening around her,
couldn't think. They were wrong about that.

Beneath the painkillers and sedatives her mind
drifted and skipped. The curare made it impossible
for her to speak. Even without the curare it was
doubtful she could have made the connections
necessary for talking. But that didn't keep her mind
from functioning.

She could still hear, she could still think. It was
fuzzy, her mind didn't want to work right. She
couldn't concentrate on anything, follow a thought
straight through. She could hear the hissing of the
respirator, the muted voices of the people around
her. Most of the time it didn't make any sense.
People moved her, said things to her in soft voices.
Occasionally something connected but she couldn't
respond. Her arms and legs were miles away, the
wires that controlled them were broken. Her mouth
wouldn't work. The hiss of air was the most soothing
sound she had ever heard.

She drifted, eyes open, unseeing.

She drifted to Kentucky, the grass was wet with morning dew. Moses. Once there was a boy, a man, a strong person she leaned upon. He was there for awhile and then he went away. The water in the lake was always cool, the mud oozed through her toes as she waded. The boys swung out over the lake on a thick vine from a tall tree. She had always wanted to do that, but it was for boys only. They often swam without suits when they thought there were no girls around. She and Carol would hide in the weeds and watch them and laugh. They looked so, so vulnerable. Once she came at night and swung on the vine. Once. . . . Once. . . .

"You're doing fine, Jodie. I'm going to move your leg a little bit. There, that's all."

That's all. . . . Once . . . once a small vegetable garden, Saturday nights at the Rt. 40 Drive-In, popcorn and beer, could never grow corn. The hiss is rhythmic, like air flowing, like water, like a boat drifting. Under the water the large coral cities, the good things to eat. Under the water was life. Small things swam by. In the flats the water was warm . . . warm. The breeze in the afternoon was warm across the fields near home, warm in the mountains above the desert. Soaring. Life was freedom in the sky. There are no enemies, only the mate at wingtip, the constant companion. There were soft things to eat. *Confinement. Evil.* At night we would return to the roost. At night it became cold . . . cold. Cold was death, the sun was life, each night must be endured. Life must go on. Moses. Popcorn. Snowballs. Moses. Life.

"I'm going to stick you with a needle, Jodie. It won't hurt at all."

Popcorn. Moses.

Ed Brown watched Sam and Wayne drift down the corridor, their hand-held lights causing shadows to rise and fall, dart here and there. They were tracing down the last of the relays and switches Sam needed. So far, everything they needed had been there. No trouble at all.

The station seemed very strange to Brown. Once it had been as familiar as the back of his hand. Not any more. It was like going back to your old home town and finding the high school replaced by a shopping center, the old baseball diamond a parking lot. Most everything in the station was familiar, but changed. Some things were missing, others moved around. The absence of lights made a big difference. Brown was used to seeing the station brightly lit, crowded with people. The only sounds he heard were Sam and Wayne talking to each other on the intercom.

Gamma II had been much smaller than the Delta series of satellites. At most, it held fifty people, most of them military at first. After the Big Blow in the Mideast, there had been a rash of disarmament talks and the emphasis in space shifted back to research. The military had mostly left by the time Brown came up. He had been the first civilian commander in space. It had been a good time for Brown, and he looked back on it fondly.

Out of curiosity he made his way back to the board room. It was a lot smaller than he remembered it. Half the gauges were gone, wires hung at crazy angles from gaping holes in the console. His light cut a hard circle of illumination wherever he flashed it. Out of reflex, he reached for the light switch on the wall, stopped at the last moment, feeling slightly ridiculous. He was glad no one had seen him. Feeling embarrassed he sat down in the chair, *his* chair. He noticed the cushion was gone. Trash littered the floor, parts of the walls. There was a little gravity here, but the spin hadn't been corrected in years. It was a real mess. He closed his eyes, could almost imagine the way it had been.

"Ed? Where are you? We've got everything."

He snapped upright, startled. "Oh. Yeah, Sam. I was just taking a look around. Be right there." He started to leave, took one last look around the room. It was just a room, full of debris and clutter. He blinked his eyes, thought of something long ago. No, the room was more than that. It had been home for awhile.

"Jodie. I'm going to change your dressings. This may sting a little bit."

It didn't sting at all. There wasn't any feeling left on that side of her face.

Sting. Stingrays. Manta rays. The mantas. Such noble animals. Like being in prison. Bars that are walls of steel and glass. Like living in a test tube. I *know* them. At times, I *am* them. Paul was . . . was something, what? He thought he could talk to the mantas. He was right? Wrong? Can't talk—*feel*! Feel the wind, I am borne skyward by the updraft. The ground tilts below me as I ride the shifting thermals. I am built to soar, to feel the rush of wind under my wings, to know the comfort of my mate beside me. Mate. Birth. Soon. Protect. Protect.

"Just this one more time, Jodie. Then we'll be through for now."

Protect mate. Reach out. Birth. Child thing. Popcorn. Protect. Moses.

*   *   *

Brown finished stowing the gear. Sam was strapping himself into his seat. Wayne was jammed in back, he couldn't move if he had to. After securing the last of the supplies, Brown palmed the hatch shut, flipped the two safety switches. He pulled himself back to the pilot's seat, started punching numbers into the computer.

The computer said no.

Brown punched some more numbers into it, asked it why.

The computer said that there was no oxygen in the spacecraft. While that was a condition that didn't particularly bother the computer, it had been programmed to give that information out. It might possibly be of interest to the people inside.

"Shit," said Brown. "We've lost our pressure somewhere." He flipped a few switches, checked the gauges. "Got to be back there," he said, pulling himself back to a panel behind Wayne. The panel fell off in his hands. It had obviously been loosened.

"What is it, Ed?" asked Sam.

"Someone's been in here," he said. "Damn oxygen line's been filed through. Probably didn't start leaking until we vented the cabin."

Wayne panicked. He tried to scramble out of the hole he'd been shoved into. Brown knocked him back down.

"Stay put, Wayne. Don't lose your head."

"But . . . my God, we're gonna—."

"We're not gonna anything," said Brown, replacing the panel. "Whoever did this didn't know beans about what he was doing. We don't have any cabin oxygen left, but there's plenty of reserve in our suits. More than enough to get us back. If he was trying to stop us, he sure blew it." He climbed back to the pilot's seat, suppressing a small shiver. If the guy had known what he was doing, they'd all be dead by now. Sam would realize that without being told. It was better not to let Wayne in on that little secret. He put an override on the computer's "no" and punched in figures for the return to Delta III. He keyed the main directional antenna into position and radioed the station.

"Delta III, this is Relay One."

"Roger, Relay One, we read you."

"We're heading home with the bacon. Suggest you find out who's been mucking around with our pride and joy."

"Relay One, this is Delta III. We copy, but do not understand."

"You don't have to understand, just send me some numbers."

"They're on their way. What the hell happened anyway?"

"Somebody tried to fuck us up. Got the numbers. We're coming home. Now."

By now they should be dead. They can not change the way things are. Machinery will breed nothing but more machinery. It is evil to tamper with the things that are as they should be. We of Earth have much to learn, many prices to pay. This is but one small one. Before we are worthy of the stars, there will be many more.

"Vital signs are down. She's slipping."

Cold. Why am I cold? I dropped the mouse. Got to find the mouse. Something funny about a mouse loose in a space station. Set a trap, bait it with cheese.

Cheese would be good, hard yellow: yellow like the sun that clears the mountains every morning, warms the desert floor. Things to eat there, food scurries in the shadows. Walls of glass and steel. Birth.

"Bicarb. Stat!"

They reach out to me, touch me with their worlds. I am the things they are, the things they were. We are one. Unity.

"Give me a hand. Hurry. Over here."

Dizzy. Like swimming down an endless pool. So dark. Everything is spinning around me.

"Move that out of the way. Zap her again, I'm not getting anything at all."

I'm alone, but I can feel the presence of others, some human, some not. I am not afraid. Dizzy. Moses. So dark. Strange, I thought it would hurt.

It doesn't hurt at all.

"She's gone."

"You did the best you—."

"Shut up!"

The manta shifted on his perch. Another thread broken. Food. Birth. He lifted into the air, spread his wings to catch the breeze.

The time of birthing meant the female could not join in the hunt for food. There was an increased need for food, an increased awareness of the furry animals that lived on the desert floor. The threads were lines to the food, to the furry animals. In the past, if he followed the threads he could always find food. Here it was different, the threads all ran to places he could not reach. It confused him.

Chapter Eight

They had settled on a pressure of 1.5 atmospheres in the sealed portion of the station. Theoretically, they could have run it up much higher than that, but there were problems.

People had to leave the sealed areas quite frequently to reach other sections of the stations. The laboratories, engineering deck, and most of the other sections maintained a normal atmosphere. To get to these places, a person first had to go through decompression. Leaving 1.5 atmospheres didn't require a very long period of decompression. At higher pressures, it took a considerable length of time. In the chamber, for instance, when they dove to 300 feet, an effective pressure of 10 atmospheres, it took five hours of decompression for each 45 minutes of exposure.

The other problem was that of oxygen toxicity. Constant exposure to pure oxygen at over 3 atmospheres could cause a variety of unpleasant symptoms, including numbness, dizziness, nausea and convulsions. There was also the danger of acute oxygen poisoning, the failure of the oxygen buffering system of hemoglobin. All in all, it wasn't a very good trade-off except in extreme circumstances.

Still, Rob felt pretty good about it. At least they had slowed down the transmission of the disease, even if they couldn't treat it.

The green light flashed at the end of the decompression chamber and Rob palmed the door open. It was very quiet outside the sealed wards, nobody went out there unless they had a reason to. A very good reason.

Rob reached his lab without passing a single person in the hall. He flipped on the light and looked with dismay at the stack of papers on his desk. He spent as much time pushing papers around as he did in actual laboratory work. He'd put so many hours in at the computer complex he felt he could almost speak ALGOL or whatever that computer language was that they used. He itched to get back to work at the microscope, but first he'd have to get rid of the papers. He'd left them stacked on top of his desk last night when he left. Why hadn't they all just disappeared or something?

No such luck. He sat in his chair and got down to business.

Linda didn't know what to do with the paper she had in her hand. It was the confidential psychological profile on Carlos Mendoza. It was quite complete.

The report had been prepared on Earth by a team of psychologists. They had made extensive use of Linda's notes, but had done quite a bit of work on their own. Most requests from Delta III got priority and fast results. They interviewed a dozen people who had worked with Carlos, his students, people who lived near him, people who were related to him. All the government files on him had been pulled. It boiled down to one thing.

Carlos Mendoza was not a very stable person.

He could not handle rejection very well and, if provoked, it was assumed he was capable of violent behavior. Fifteen years ago, he had been arrested on a charge of aggravated assault, but the details were fuzzy. The charge had been dropped when the other party, a woman, refused to file a formal complaint. For what it was worth, the report also mentioned that he had once thrown a plate of food at a colleague during a lunchroom argument over an experiment.

Carlos was judged to be eccentric and unstable. Otherwise, he was intelligent and well trained, quite suitable for his role as a research scientist. The unstated implication in the report was that a little eccentricity was not an altogether undesirable quality for such a scientist.

Linda had requested the information because she had suspected some sort of a personality change in Carlos. It had only been a vague suspicion, nothing really concrete. It wasn't unusual; most of the people on the station were having trouble of one sort or another trying to cope with the nearly unbearable situation. Now, this report. Again, there was nothing she could pin down, just a bad feeling about the whole thing. He hadn't kept his appointment with Candy, continued to put it off whenever she tried to reschedule it.

This whole thing might be nothing at all, and

Linda rather hoped that was the case. If so, bringing it to anyone's attention would be doing Carlos a grave disservice. On the other hand, if it was important, she had a duty to inform the proper people.

It was a hard decision for her to make. Due to the confidential nature of the problem, there wasn't anyone she could talk it over with. She paced the room for awhile, mulling it over. Finally, she made up her mind. She went to the screen and punched the numbers that would connect her with the captain.

He was very interested in what she had to say.

Otis Weekfield couldn't take it any more. This time Greer had gone too far. He threw the newspaper across the room, got up and walked to the window. It was snowing in Washington, the city just starting to stir for the morning. His window looked out over the Potomac River. A small boat moved through the water in the swirling snow.

All over the city, people would be reading their morning paper, tearing newsfax sheets from their home computer terminals. They carried the same headline. After all, it isn't often there's a suicide in the White House. At 11:18 pm last night, James K. Blassiter had blown the side of his head away in the oval office. He had been in conference with the President and two of his aides. They had tried to stop him, but failed.

Sixty-five years old. Forty years of public service. Weekfield hadn't really cared for Blassiter personally, but that didn't matter. He deserved better than that. He was an old man and somebody pushed him. Arnold Greer pushed him, killed him as surely as if it had been his finger on the trigger. Greer had stepped over the line a couple times before, but as far as Otis was concerned, this was the last straw. He had to be stopped.

Otis walked back to his desk and unlocked his file drawer. He took all the papers out and dumped them on the floor. Then he pried off the false bottom and removed the three sheets of paper he'd hidden there.

The information on those three sheets of paper had cost him plenty, and not just in terms of money. In a way it had cost him his wife and son, dead in an automobile accident that hadn't really been an accident. The only reason he was still alive was that he had carefully leaked information that gave the impression he had given up on this particular project, that he couldn't fit the pieces together. But he had it all here in his hand now—names, dates, places. Everything in it could be proven. Greer was just a pawn in the overall picture, he probably didn't have any idea he was being manipulated. But he'd topple right along with the rest of them.

It was big, very big, and messy as hell. It hit two of the largest corporations in the country, tied them in with a group of African nations and a block of Eastern European governments. They wanted control of space, and they wanted it bad. By backing Greer, the two U.S. corporations would have been able to put whatever they wanted into orbit under the guise of freedom of enterprise. What they would have put into orbit would have been deadly. Otis had a microfiche of one of their designs. It was a killer.

Otis was tired. Tired of people bending other people to suit their needs. Tired of watching and walking through webs of deceit. Tired of the wrong people doing the wrong things at the wrong times.

He didn't kid himself, though. This wouldn't solve

everything, but it would knock a lot of people down. It would be worth it. Maybe.

As he slid the first sheet of blank paper into his typewriter, he felt he was driving nails into his coffin. This would bother a lot of very dangerous people.

The snow was still falling, slower now. Traffic would be a mess this morning. Washington just couldn't handle snow with any dignity at all. As the typewriter clacked in the book-lined room, Otis felt like he was typing his obituary.

They couldn't find Carlos. He wasn't in the sealed part of the station, that they knew for sure. That was about all they knew for sure. Bounds and his security team had swept the rest of the station twice without any result. It was a big station.

Sam sat in one of the chairs in the engineering room. He was by himself; half working, half taking it easy. The big rush of work had been over by the time they had sealed up the wards. It had been interesting, a lot of different things to do. They'd had to do a lot of rewiring, revamp most of the air supply network. The old airlocks had to be moved around, made operational again. It was a challenge and had kept them pretty busy for awhile. Now they were more or less idle again and Sam didn't like it.

He didn't like to sit around with nothing to do. It made him nervous, gave him time to think about things he didn't like to think about. Like that virus thing.

All he was doing now was watching the gauges and they hardly ever changed. His end of the station was moving smoothly. He should have been proud, but he wasn't. He'd rather have something happen to keep him busy. He yawned.

The station breathes through this man. He is evil. He works with machinery, not living things. He cannot feel the life beyond. He is like the others, the ones who went in the ship. He would change the way things are, the way things ought to be. I failed before. I will not fail this time.

Sam put his feet up on the console, tried to relax. He didn't understand all this talk about virus stuff. Maybe he'd have Wayne give him a hand tomorrow and they could pull the sub-damper from the auxiliary power system. Nothing really wrong with it, but it hadn't been bench-tested in three months and was due for a check. Give them something to do, anyway. He noticed the bubble on the flow-by valve was stuck again and leaned forward to tap it loose. As he did that, he heard something click behind him. What the hell?

It happened quickly. Sam could have stopped him easily except that he was sitting in an awkward position in the chair, feet up on the console. As it was, he managed to twist a little to his left. The pipe caught him on the shoulder and the chair slipped out from under him, dumping him on the floor. He rolled as far away as quickly as he could, ending up against a wire mesh wall.

Sam got to his feet, but he was off balance as the man charged, swinging the pipe in an arc towards his head. No time for anything fancy. Sam just ducked under the swing and dove out of the way.

The man couldn't stop the swing. The heavy pipe crashed through the protective wire mesh to the machinery behind. Twenty-four thousand volts zapped through the metal bar.

Carlos Mendoza froze, every muscle in his body rigid.

Sparks flew from the wall. The smell of smoke and burning flesh filled the room.

Sam picked up the chair and swung it at Carlos, knocking him away from the wall.

By then he was dead.

Arnold Greer couldn't believe what he was reading. Otis might go out on a limb once in awhile, but not like this. If one tenth of what he said was true, then the last twenty years of his life had been a joke. And Greer had a sinking feeling that everything in the article was true. It was much too complete, had too many details to have been faked.

Mike Hickson sat in a chair across the room, his head in his hands. He'd been with Greer a long time, they'd been through a lot together. It looked like it was finished.

Greer thought it over. All the years of scrambling, manipulating, pulling himself up a rung at a time; it all came down to this. He'd been someone else's patsy. A fall guy. Manipulated to a degree he'd never in his wildest imagination thought possible.

All his dreams were ashes in his mouth.

Greer went to the vidphone, punched through to an Earth line, gave the operator a number. After a few minutes Mark Owens came on the screen. He looked shaken.

"Is it true, Mark? Give it to me straight."

Owens nodded. "I'm afraid so."

"Goddamn it."

The screen went blank. There really wasn't anything left to say.

So this is what it's like, thought Linda as she walked through the wards, *to grow old, to lose so many things.* She paused at the foot of a bed, picked up the clipboard, read the lab results. The numbers swam before her eyes, ran together. They didn't appear to make any sense. Why had they run a brain scan on this person? What did these results mean? They could be normal for all she knew. She dropped the clipboard. It swung on its chain, clanked softly against the bed frame.

The patient was in serious condition, that much she was sure of. Eyes glazed, he stared dully at her with no sign of comprehension. He breathed with great difficulty, drawing in air with irregular spastic gasps. He had been in the chamber earlier and was scheduled to go back in another two hours. It would help a little.

It all helped a little, nothing helped very much. Time was running out for all of them.

She pushed her cart among the beds, reading the medication cards, administering the proper doses. She was accompanied on her rounds today by Per Anson, a first-rate mechanic. He knew everything there was to know about wrenches. He knew next to nothing about medicine. As she read the cards, he looked over her shoulder. He read the labels on the tubes she selected from the cart. He double checked everything she did. Proper patient, proper medication, proper dosage. He read them out loud: "Curare, 10cc." His voice echoed against the muted background of gasping patients and the monotonous thump and wheeze of the respirators. Always the sounds of rushing oxygen, gurgling through the humidifiers, gently pumped into dying lungs. Always the smell, the feel of death.

He nodded, she administered the meds, they both signed the chart. It was standard procedure these days, a constant guard against errors, mistakes. And still so many slipped by. She had made a few herself, none serious. Soon there would be too many mistakes and it would be all over.

The patients had been friends, acquaintances. You knew everything about everybody in a place this small. Now they were just bodies, numbers on a chart. The faces were familiar, but changed. A filter had slid down behind their eyes, taking something essential away. They were no longer people she had known, they were bodies giving up life day by day.

She stopped at the last bed in the row. Susan Walker, head nurse. She was shaking as she prepared the meds. There seemed to be so little hope.

They finished, stripped off their isolation suits, and went through the decontamination hallway. It usually took at least an hour for the decontamination procedure and Linda felt it was a massive waste of time. Surely by now they were all infected to some extent. She and Per sat on benches opposite each other. Suited figures came and went, did things to their bodies. They sat in silence. They were lost in their own thoughts, there was nothing new to say.

She dozed, dreamed of Earth and running free. It was wrong. All the places were wrong, jumbled. She was a child in places she had lived as an adult. She got a strong image of a street in Sweden, though she'd never been there. Without knowing why or how, the street was familiar. Other streets flashed by, a dirt road to a deserted cabin. Blisters. She had been . . . how old? A desert stretched out below her. Mantas. Who was it? Paul, that's it. He thought he could read the mantas' minds. Strange. She could feel the hot sun. Not words, not precisely images, either. Just a kind of feeling. Food, something to do

with food. The hunt. A strong male image. Birth.
She felt dizzy, confused. The hot sun made her
sleepy. She wanted to curl up on the sand. Sand?
Something was slipping from her. Paul is dead now.
A dog named Skippy licked her face, became Rob in
the dark with a messy kiss. She stirred, sat up,
pressed her back against the cold wall. Her eyes were
closed. How old was she when she lived in Greenbelt.
Had she *ever* lived in Greenbelt? She couldn't be
sure. She thought she had, but there weren't many
memories to go with it. A cedar cabin, a motel room
over the ocean. There were more memories attached
to Sweden than Greenbelt. That's silly—she'd never
been . . . never been . . . Sweden? She felt half asleep.
That was it, she was asleep. No, awake. Half awake.
So tired. She looked up, saw Rob. It was good to see
him. She wanted to open her arms to him, have him
hold her. Rob- . . . no, not Rob . . . Per. Per was
from Sweden. What was happening? She tried to
stand, lost her footing, slipped, fell on the metal
floor. *Rob! Oh God, please, Rob, please.* Per
jumped away in horror. Suited figures carried her
back into the ward. They put her in bed next to
Susan.

More threads came and went, yet they were never
linked to food he could see. Nervously, he circled the
enclosure. The birthing had started. There wasn't
much time.

Chapter Nine

Papers filled his desk, overflowed into loose stacks on the floor. Rob went over his data for the tenth time; slowly, methodically. It was too late in the game for a mistake. A break. At last.

This morning's slides sat by the microscope. Ninety-seven slides to match the ninety-seven deep-agar cultures in the lab. The results were the same as yesterday: 95 positive for the presence of the organism and the same two, numbers 42 and 43, negative. The two were cultures from Jodie Pope. She had been infected before she died, heavily infected. But something significant had happened before she died. She had been producing antibodies against the organism. If she hadn't been attacked, she might have pulled through without any sign of the disease at all. That was the first sign of any effective defense mechanism. At least it worked in some people. Who? And to what degree?

Rob thought he might have a handle on the

"who," though it wasn't much. Cross-checking medical backgrounds between Jodie and the other victims in this particular group showed that she was the only female with both an Rh-negative factor and a positive Rubella titer. She was also the only one who had produced antibodies. It was circumstantial, tenuous. It was their only break.

Checking medical records, Rob had come up with four other women on the station with similar profiles. Two were already dead. That left Eng-Lai, communications officer, and Linda. As things stood, their antibody systems probably wouldn't even be enough to save themselves, but Rob had a plan. He was sure Ground Control wouldn't like it. Riggs would never permit it and Eng-Lai wouldn't go behind the captain's back.

That left Linda.

Riggs filled the screen. Rob was nervous, but tried hard not to show it. He had to give it his best shot.

"Run that by me again, will you, Rob?" asked Riggs.

"I'm going to try to cultivate antibodies against the organism. It'll take time, but I think it can be done."

"How? I didn't think you could even culture the organism."

"We can't, not in the quantities we need. I'm proposing an *in vivo* method of producing the antibodies."

"*In vivo*? What do you mean by that?"

"*In vivo* means within the living organism as opposed to culture methods. If we expose a suitable individual to a high-enough level of infection there's a chance we might trigger the body to produce antibodies in sufficient quantities not only to save their own life, but others.''

"You want to *infect* people? Have you gone crazy on us?''

"I believe it's the only way we can get at it. If we pass a certain level of infection, it's possible we'll reach a threshold where the body will continue producing antibodies in quantity. Perhaps a sufficient quantity to pull the rest of us through.''

"You don't know for sure this will work, do you?''

"The evidence for it is circumstantial, I admit. The threshold theory is only a hypothesis. I believe it's our only answer.''

"I suppose you've talked this over with the scientists at Ground Control. What's their opinion?''

Rob grimaced. "They're against it, sir. They believe the risk factor is too high for such a low probability of success.''

"You don't agree with them?''

"No. *No!* They're playing this thing far too conservatively. We're the ones taking the risk. We ought to be able to decide for ourselves how much of a risk we are willing to take.''

"I'm inclined to think they're right in this instance,'' said Riggs. "It doesn't sound to me like you have very much to go on.''

"It's *all* we have to go on.''

"There must be other aspects to explore. Besides, if you can't cultivate the organism, how do you propose to collect enough to inoculate these people?''

"Collect them directly from the male manta.''

"No. Absolutely not. I've had the mantas sealed,

isolated. They are not to be approached for any reason. Damn buzzards, they're the cause of all this trouble. No one goes near them. We can't take the chance."

"It may be our only chance. Time is running out."

"That's enough, Rob. Don't try to push me. Ground Control's against it, I'm against it. It's finished, closed. Forget it."

Rob nodded, the screen went blank. He wasn't about to forget it.

Everything seemed so far away. Linda could hear sounds but she couldn't put them together right. Bottles clanking became music, the gaps filled by the hissing of pumped air, the gurgling of water. She floated, drifted. It was like being asleep on a boat in the gulf on a warm day, no waves, the water as smooth as a piece of glass. She could almost feel the sun. She had trouble breathing, felt like she was suffocating. She would try to gasp for breath, but none came. Her arms and legs felt impossibly far away, she couldn't be sure if they were moving or not. She had trouble concentrating, following a thought through. She had felt this way when she had her wisdom teeth pulled. Teeth. How can a tooth have wisdom? The dentist was young and smiled too much. It was a long time ago, or maybe yesterday.

"Where are her lab results?"

"Right here, Doctor."

"This seems a little high. I want an hourly glucose and B.U.N. on this patient. Keep an eye on it."

"Yes, Doctor."

Hollow. The voices were hollow, they echoed from the end of some long, dark tunnel. The things they said made no sense, they seemed to be syllables thrown together in some random fashion. Everything had a soft red glow. There were memories, things to hold on to. Rob. A dog. Distant places, familiar things. The beat of leathery wings. The pain of birth. Pain. Hunger. A cedar cabin with the night-wings of owls. A snow-covered campus, huddled against the wind, ten minutes to change classes, across the quadrangle of swirling snow. Cold outside, the labs were too hot, thirty bunsen burners going at the same time, the smell of organic compounds, hard to breathe. Rob. Try to breathe. *Oh damn*. Hot. Bunsen burners, desert sun. Hunger. Search for food. Leathery wings. A long, white, sandy beach. Holding hands. Sharing important things. Sharing trivial things. Laughing. Crying. An old psychology professor, rumpled suit, making rats do things they didn't want to do. White coats. Nursing school. Thousands of injections. Susan. White rats. Unhappy white rats. Neurotic white rats. We are all rats in cages, each with our very own personal treadmill that someone else designed. Rob. Rob? Hot desert/hot desert/hot desert/hot sun/hot sun. Laughing on a lazy day. A storm rolling in off the gulf, huge billowing clouds, crashing thunder echoes over the water, sharp lightning flashes. White lightning/white nurse's caps/white rats/white snowballs. Snowballs. Unfolding, searching warmth, food. Always food. Lines reach out to me. Food? it asks. No. Am not food, am person. Person? Like . . . like. . . . How can it be explained? Take all the things from birth to death, put them one after another, each breath, each action, everything done or not done; add them all together. A person, a life, a very special thing, something worth saving. Where is Rob? How I want him. Maybe he's here and I can't feel it. There are so many things I can't feel, can't do. What has happened to me? I remember the dog. I remember Sweden, too. A funny-shaped country on a map. Full of narrow streets, cats, dogs, people living out their lives. A warm fireplace, chopping wood, blisters.

"Increase her Demerol drip. Keep her a little further down. It can't hurt her."

"Yes, Doctor."

Doctors and dentists. Things that hurt, things that heal. Things that never heal. So much scar tissue on my soul. Regrets. I would do *this* differently if I could do it all over again, I would change *that*. So many things that never heal. I would be a better person, I would be the same person. I want a chance. Sailing with Rob, sharing a warm beer. The time the car broke down and he fixed it with a rope and two coat hangers. We missed the concert, but found something else. Hand in hand through the pine woods, the needles a thick, bouncy bed underfoot. It was nice. I know his face as well as I know my own. His touch is soft: long fingers: he should have been a piano player: hours of practicing chords, scales: long fingers: on my arm: my body: strong fingers. Coasting on thermals, feeling the freedom of wind and sky. The urge to protect. Hunger. We did so much together. We never did enough together.

"Doctor, are those tears?"

"Yes. They're automatic, though. They don't mean a thing."

Oh, Rob. Rob!

Rob decompressed with the crew that was leaving the nursing quarters to pick up the latest shuttle shipment. His presence there was not unusual, since he often went back and forth to his lab. As soon as the cycle finished, Rob separated from the crew. He headed straight for the mantas, stopping only once on the way to pick up a general issue suit from the lockers.

The seal on the entrance chamber to the mantas' enclosure was a complicated device that would only open by the insertion of a specially magnetized key. It would take hours with sophisticated equipment to jimmy the lock. He solved the problem in three seconds by the scientific application of a short piece of pipe.

He switched to internal support, put on the suit's helmet and vented the chamber. When it had filled with the manta's atmosphere and adjusted to the pressure, he opened the far door and stepped inside.

The mantas were excited. The female was squawking, thrashing around on her perch, her swollen belly a mass of deep, raw gashes. Rob could see movement of the baby manta inside. It would be born soon, fully formed, ready to fly, eat, kill.

The male was flying protectively around the female, large talons unsheathed, green eyes rolling wildly. The air was hazy with mist. Butterflies scattered. Life, birth, death: everything merged.

Rob set his bag down, removed a slender glass tube with a hypodermic needle on the end. He would have to get close enough to the male manta to reach one of the secreting sacs that covered its belly like large warts.

As he approached the mantas, the male attacked. Rob spun out of the way, grabbed one of its legs and twisted the manta to the floor. It flapped awkwardly, beating Rob with its massive wings. Rob juggled the glass tube into position. As he plunged the needle in, the manta jerked, its talons ripping Rob's suit.

Rob gasped, choked on the sudden inrush of caustic fumes. His throat burned, his nose stung. His eyes clouded over with a thin white film. He could feel blood running down the inside of his suit. His only concern was to hold onto the tube and get the hell out of there.

He made his way to the door on his knees, the tube cradled protectively against his chest. The manta swung into the air, circled, dove at him. It raked Rob's back with its sharp talons. Rob no longer had the strength to resist. The helmet, at least, protected his head. He was giddy, his time sense blown all apart. It seemed like hours of pain, it was only seconds. The cool air was rushing into the chamber before Rob realized he had reached it safely. While the exchange process was being completed, he removed his useless suit, tore his shirt into strips and tried to stop the worst of the bleeding. He inserted the glass tube into a sterile syringe, and when the outer door opened, he headed back across the ship to the wards.

It was a long trip, painful. The empty rooms and corridors amplified every noise he made. He could hear the humming of distant machinery, the constant hiss of air circulating. He felt removed, alone, isolated. His head swam. Weak. Lost a lot of blood. Massive infection, surely a fatal dose.

He floated across the zero-g section, a solitary figure dwarfed by the massive room. A slowly rotating flyspeck.

The rest was uphill. He fought the increasing gravity every foot of the way. By the time he reached the decompression chamber outside the wards, he was exhausted.

When the cycle finished he staggered into the nursing quarters. He was immediately surrounded by men who warily advanced toward him. Obviously his encounter had been monitored. Riggs had probably been seized by a fit of apoplexy. At what—the danger? Or the breach of his precious regulations?

Everything moved in slow motion for Rob. His blood pounded in his ears. The men moved awkwardly, like puppets on unsure strings. They were afraid to touch him, and for good reason, too. Even at 1.5 atmospheres, skin contact was sufficient for transfer of the infection and he was a walking Typhoid Mary.

He waved the loaded syringe in front of him like a knife. The men parted uncertainly, opening a path towards the wards. He waited for one of them to pull a hero act, but no one tried anything. They had seen too many friends die too slowly. People were suiting up, shouting conflicting orders at each other.

Linda lay in a bed in the middle of the crowded ward. She tried to move, fought the restraints that bound her arms and legs. Bottles clanked on rods above her bed. Her eyes focused on Rob, but there was nothing behind them, no love, no recognition. Only pain and the single-minded desire to be free from all the things that hurt.

Rob moved her sweat-soaked sheets aside. So thin, pale. Tears came to his eyes. Love, life, death; everything mixed, intermingled.

Thirty-five cc's, he thought, trying to drive his mind from other things. *Intraperitoneally*. He swabbed an area just below her navel.

Choking back a sob, he inserted the needle.

"Forgive me," he said. Three men in suits were crashing through the ward.

"I love you," he said as he pushed the plunger, injecting the deadly spawn of a windswept world. He had made the decision, taken the chance. It was over now. He had either killed the person he loved or saved her life. He had sealed everyone's fate; they would live or die according to what happened in Linda's body. He would likely never know.

By the time the three men reached him, he had collapsed to the floor.

Hours, days, weeks, they all ran together for Rob. He drifted in and out of varying degrees of consciousness. Real and unreal images blurred and shifted. He thought he was dying several times over and one day he opened his eyes and there was Linda. *Linda!*

She touched his hair, put her finger to his mouth.

"Hush," she said. "Don't try to talk."

That part was easy. His mouth felt like it was stuffed with cotton. He was thirsty as hell.

"You were right, Rob. Eng-Lai and I are regular little antibody factories. We've got it under control now. You're one of the last to come around. Of course, you always were kind of slow." She laughed, sat on the edge of the bed.

"We've got to get you out of here soon. Lots of work ahead for us. You're the world's number-one authority on the manta menace and they expect to have a rough time back on Earth. Two shifts rotated down before the quarantine."

"Mantas," whispered Rob. "I dreamed—."

"It was no dream," said Linda. "We all went

through it. It seems to be tied in somehow with the manta's search for food. A kind of a mental link between living organisms. Some people feel it more than others. It mostly goes away after you recover, but not entirely. I have the feeling that this may be the most significant thing to come out of all this.''

Rob nodded, trying to take it all in at once. He looked at Linda's eyes, felt deep emotions stirring. She squeezed his hand and suddenly he wasn't thirsty anymore.

In another part of the station, Riggs monitored the mantas that had turned 3000 metric tons of precision equipment into an orbiting tin can of death. One hundred and thirty-two people died.

The small manta—the baby—moved slightly, caught Riggs' attention. Two green eyes—cold, hard—rotated slowly, endlessly searching for a sandy horizon they would never see.